The Math Inspectors 4

THE CASE OF THE HAMILTON ROLLER COASTER

By
DANIEL KENNEY
&
EMILY BOEVER

Thanks to:
Sumit Roy for his fantastic illustrations, Jerry Dorris for
another great cover design, Cassie Leaders
(CassieLeaders@gmail.com) for her proof reading, and
the always fantastic Jason Anderson (Polgarus Studio)
for another great job formatting our books!

To my brothers.

Daniel Kenney

To Jaime, my very first partner in crime. What adventures we have had!

Emily Boever

TABLE OF CONTENTS

CHAPTER ONE

THE FIRST DAY OF SUMMER

Stanley looked at the clock. "We're not going to make it," he said.

23 seconds left.

"Dude," said Felix, "just choose one. The red or the blue? Let's go."

"But I have no way of knowing which one to choose," said Stanley.

"Well, we have 19 seconds to decide. Don't over think it—just go with your gut!"

Stanley examined his choices again. Red or blue? "I hate going with my gut."

"Good point," said Felix. "If there is anybody's gut we should be going with, it's mine."

Felix grabbed the blue one, turned to Gertie, and prepared for the worst.

10 seconds left.

"What are you waiting for?" Gertie screamed.

"Do it!" yelled Charlotte.

7 seconds left. Now 6. Now 5.

"Are you sure?" asked Felix.

"Do it, Felix!" said Gertie. "Do it now!"

3...2...

Felix raised his hand and hesitated for a moment. Then he cracked the blue egg over Gertie's head.

1!

A buzzer blared. And the crowd exploded in laughter as thick yellow yoke oozed down Gertie's face.

"Nicely done, gut boy," growled Gertie, yanking a handkerchief from Felix's hand.

"Hey, don't be too hard on my tummy," he said. "It hasn't failed me since that whole cheese-on-chocolate anchovy disaster. And that was over a year ago."

Stanley looked up at the sign over the amusement park booth they were standing at and read it again.

Dr. Know-It-All, Riddleologist Extraordinaire!
Match Your Wits Against My Genius, If You Dare...
Everybody Wins! Incredible Prizes!
Price: Two Tickets. Riddles For All Sizes.

"But it wasn't a riddle," said Stanley to the man behind the booth. Dr. Know-It-All wore a black suit, red bow tie, and a very tall top hat. He was medium height and medium build. Everything about him seemed medium, now that Stanley thought about it, with the exception of a long mustache that was waxed into a fancy spiral on each cheek.

Dr. Know-It-All pulled at his right mustache and smiled. "I assure you, young man, it was quite fair. I presented you with two eggs. Your challenge was to riddle out which one was real and which one was the imposter. You had 60 seconds to decide. And you had to test your choice by cracking the egg over a volunteer's head. You riddled, you cracked, and unfortunately for the brave young lady here, you chose incorrectly."

"It was all worth it for the prize," said Gertie, looking at the boxes of valuable gadgets lining the back shelves of the booth. "Let's see, I'll take the nice shiny silver smart tablet, please. Unless you have one in pink."

Dr. Know-It-All laughed. "But you did not solve the riddle, my dear."

Herman pointed at the sign. "It says everybody wins."

"And so it does," said the man. "Everybody does win something. Either a prize on the shelves back there or a prize even more valuable: knowledge. You, my young friends, have won knowledge. You now know which egg was real and which was not."

"Wait," said Charlotte, picking up the red egg. "How do we know both eggs weren't real? That way, you'd win every time."

The man pointed at the counter between them and smiled. "Be my guest."

Charlotte drew the red egg back and knocked it twice against the counter. She put both thumbs inside the crack and pulled the shell apart. There, perched in the open egg, was the tiniest bird any of them had ever seen. It was jet black except for bright red spots on the tips of its wings. Charlotte tried to close her hands around it, but the bird darted away toward the nearest tree.

"How did you do that?" Gertie asked Dr. Know-It-All.

"Forgive me if I do not divulge trade secrets," he said. "All I can tell you is that no birds were harmed in the making of my riddles. No foul business with my fowls, you might say."

"But it *wasn't* a riddle," Stanley said, a little more forcefully this time. "The kids before us had 60 seconds to solve a logic puzzle. And the kids before them had 60 seconds to figure out the Tower of Hanoi. Which we could do in our sleep. *Those* were riddles. *Ours* was not. Choose an egg? How? The eggs were completely similar in height and weight, at least as far as I could tell. They felt the same when you shook them, and both spun on their sides instead of their tops. The only difference between them was their color. That's not a riddle—that's a guessing game."

"Yeah," said Felix, "and who ever heard of a *Doctor* Know-It-All, anyway? Whatever happened to just plain old *Mister* Know-It-All?"

The man shrugged. "I was the first person in my

family to go to college. Now, because you kids have been such good sports, I will give you one more piece of knowledge, free of charge: Not all riddles can be solved with your brains—sometimes you just have to choose and hope for the best. Sometimes, a riddle is just a riddle."

"Thanks for that golden nugget of wisdom," said Gertie. "But I'd rather have the tablet. I'm starting to wonder how many of those you've actually given away."

Dr. Know-It-All smiled again. "A grand total of zero. I am, after all, a genius. But it is time for me to close things up for lunch, and time for you to go enjoy the rest of the afternoon. Do I understand correctly that this is your first day of summer vacation as well as being the opening day of the amusement park?"

"That's right," said Charlotte. "Hamilton Park opens up every year the day after school ends. It's a tradition."

"And what a tradition!" said Felix. "For one glorious day kids get in free, rides are free, and all the cotton candy you can stuff in your face is free. Which I'll attempt to go easy on, seeing as how I'm a heavy favorite in the funnel cake eating contest this afternoon."

Dr. Know-It-All tipped his top hat. "I see I am not the only one with much ado. Let us follow the example of our little bird friend, then, and be about our way." With that he nodded good-bye, and the crowd began to disperse. He pulled a rope, and a big wooden board slid down to cover the booth window. A sign on the front of it read: *Out To Lunch.*

"He is a little *out to lunch*," said Gertie.

"It wasn't a fair riddle," said Stanley.

Charlotte slapped him on the back. "Don't let it ruin your day."

"Yeah, Stanley," said Gertie. "I know three little words that'll cheer you right up. Hamilton Roller Coaster. Or is rollercoaster one word?"

"Typically you find it as two words," came the answer. "And that is the way it is listed in the dictionary; although, it is not incorrect to spell it as one word in common usage. So, you should probably omit the space."

Gertie spun around to find the voice and glared up into the face of a strikingly pretty girl. "Maybe you should exit this space, Polly Partridge. This is a private conversation."

Polly was at the point of responding when her scowl transformed into a smile. "It seems I am not the only one around here who thinks you Math Nerds are getting cocky. Someone else decided you needed a little egg on your face, huh? In that case our work here is done, ladies and gents." The group of English snobs behind Polly gave a snort of approval.

Polly checked her watch. "Almost time for the main event, Stanley. May the best team win. It looks like you have just enough time to get in a kiddie ride, if you hurry." The English Club laughed again and walked away.

"How well she knows me," sighed Felix.

"Hold still, Gertie," said Charlotte. "Come here a second. You turned so red I think the egg started to scramble in your hair."

"My sweet Polly is right about the time," continued Felix. "We have just enough, if we hurry. Who's with me? Let's get our Creepy on!"

Charlotte sighed and looked at Stanley. "You

know he isn't going to stop talking about it until he rides it."

"Fine," said Stanley, "let's get it over with."

Stanley, Charlotte, Gertie, Felix, and Herman walked around the corner and stopped in front of a rundown children's ride. It was a miniature roller coaster with a small circular track that had three gently sloping drops. The lead car was in the shape of an enormous clown's head with a gigantic red nose attached to the front of it and a sinister smile painted across its lower half. Each of the four trail cars was shaped like a tiny VW Bug. The cars sat motionless, and the line to ride was completely empty.

As they neared the entry, an eerie scream blared from a speaker in the clown's enormous nose: "Ha ha haaaa! Come and ride me, kids. It'll be FUN! Ha, ha, haaaa!" Two small children walking by with their parents turned and ran away crying.

"That might be the creepiest thing I've ever seen," said Herman. "Or heard."

"Apparently it didn't start out that way," said Stanley. "My parents said back in the day, before it lost most of its paint, and the speaker didn't sound like it had been swallowed by your worst nightmare, this was one of the most popular rides at the park. But time has not been good to Beepy the Clown, and it's now known to kids everywhere as Creepy the Clown."

"Why do they keep it open?" asked Herman. "Nobody in their right mind would ride that thing."

"But not everybody is in their right mind," said Gertie, jerking a thumb at Felix who stood resting his elbows on the fence and his head in his hands, staring wistfully at the ride.

Herman looked at Creepy again. "So, they keep this thing open just for Felix?"

"No," said Gertie. "For the principle of the thing. Mr. Hamilton won't close anything, no matter what. He said as long as a Hamilton runs the park, every kid should be able to enjoy it just as it's always been."

"That's why we have the oldest wooden roller coaster in the country," said Stanley. "It's a National Historic Landmark, you know?"

"Yes, Stanley," said Gertie. "We know."

"An excellent example of early twentieth-century craftsmanship."

"Yes, Stanley," said Charlotte. "We know."

"I love that roller coaster."

"Well then," Gertie smiled, "maybe this is the year you actually ride it."

Stanley lifted his pointer finger in the air. "You don't always have to ride a ride to love a ride."

"And sometimes you do," said Felix, turning to Herman. "Come on, Little Buddy, it's your first time at the park. You have to ride Creepy with me if you want the full effect."

"Ha, ha, haaaa!" screeched the clown's nose.

"I'll pass," said Herman.

Felix tossed him his phone. "Suit yourself. Here, take a picture of me then. I have one every year since I was a year old. Take a look."

Herman scrolled through a folder of pictures in Felix's phone marked *Me_Creepy*. The first was of a tiny red-headed kid, barely able to sit up by himself, sitting in the lead car and clinching the safety bar with two tiny hands. The pictures gradually changed, ending with a six-foot red-headed kid wedged into the same car.

"All I see in this last one are arms and knees," said Herman. "Are you sure he fits?"

"We almost had to use a can opener to get him out last year," said Gertie.

Felix scampered up the ramp and weaved back and forth through the sharp turns of the empty queue.

"You know you can just come through here," said the attendant, holding the exit gate open from her chair.

Felix shook his head. "Can't break with tradition," he said. Then, after a short struggle, he took his place in the clown car, clinched the safety bar with both large hands, and screamed, "Let 'er rip!"

The attendant hit a button and a bell sounded. The tiny roller coaster chugged to life and crept slowly up the first hill. It lost momentum steadily and almost came to a complete stop just as it reached the top, but it finally crested the hill and its lone rider threw his hands in the air.

As he glided around the turns, Felix bellowed in unison with Creepy's nose, "Ha, ha, haaaa!" Herman clicked away with the phone. After four circuits the bell rang again and the coaster creaked to a stop.

Felix whirled a finger over his head. "Again," he shouted.

"Hold up, Sue," Stanley yelled to the attendant. "Felix, we have to get to the stage now."

"Just once more time," Felix pleaded.

Stanley pointed just over Felix's head to the

jumbo screen visible from almost everywhere in the amusement park. The others looked and saw a live shot of several important looking people gathering on the stage.

"Fine," said Felix, wriggling out of the car. "Duty calls. Thanks for the ride, Sue. Where do they have you the rest of the day?"

"Now that you've done your thing?" said the girl. "I'm helping out at balloon darts. Thanks for coming early. Last year you made me wait all day."

"Good things come to those who wait," said Felix. "But from the look on Stanley's face, we're done waiting. See you next year."

The kids ran towards the center of the amusement park where the stage was set at the far end of a large open square. The screen showed a close-up of Mr. Hamilton, President of the Amusement Park, who was giving a speech. Behind him stood Dr. Cooling, Principal of Ravensburg Middle School.

"Wasn't this thing supposed to start at 10?" said Gertie.

"Looks like it started early," said Charlotte.

"Think we can sneak in the back unnoticed?"

"Nope," said Herman, pointing.

Stanley looked up and saw his own face filling the jumbo screen.

"And there they are now," beamed the voice of Mr. Hamilton over the loudspeakers. "Math Inspectors, please come up on stage and join the other nominees of the Hamilton Park Award."

CHAPTER TWO

AND THE WINNER IS...

"Smile, Stanley," said Gertie. "Your face is the main attraction all over the park right now."

A good sized crowd had gathered in the square, and they all started clapping for the Math Inspectors. Everyone between them and the stage cleared a path. Some people shook their hands. Others snapped selfies as they walked by. One red-headed girl even asked Felix for an autograph.

"Stanley," yelled someone in the crowd. "Hey, Stanley, wait up."

A boy stepped into the makeshift path and walked up to them. He was Blaise Brown, a friend from school who was in the Science Club.

"Hey, Blaise, how's it going?"

"Look guys, I know you're busy. And I know you solve big crimes now and probably don't have time for little things like this, but I promised my sister I'd give this to you." He held out an envelope to Stanley.

"No, no, no," said Gertie. "We have a process for this. If you want to be put on the docket, you can schedule an appointment just like everybody else. Our next opening is in three weeks from now."

"It's just that—" began Blaise.

"Come by the tree house tomorrow," said Stanley as he tried to hand the envelope back.

But Blaise didn't take it. "I get it," he said. "You're famous now. At least I can say I knew you back when." Then he stepped back into the crowd.

Mr. Hamilton was waving at them. "That's right, kids," he said. "Come up and join us."

Stanley, Charlotte, Gertie, Felix, and Herman climbed the steps on the side of the stage and were escorted to where a group of kids their own age sat. The Math Inspectors claimed the five empty seats and scanned the crowd.

"My parents are going to be bummed they missed this," whispered Gertie. "I told them it started at 10.

I don't see them anywhere."

"Mine neither," Stanley whispered back.

"As I was saying," said Mr. Hamilton to the crowd. "There are those who think our amusement park needs to change. And some who say that, with such an old man running the show, change is impossible." The crowd laughed and Mr. Hamilton laughed along with them. "Well, maybe I do like tradition," he said. "Maybe I cherish the feel of this old place. Maybe I love her old rides. But I'll admit, sometimes change is good. And that's why this year I've started a new tradition: The Hamilton Park Award."

Applause rang out.

"As you know, kids are nominated by you, the community. Kids who have shown great character and a heart for service. This year we've narrowed the choice down to four groups, each one worthy of winning."

More applause.

Mr. Hamilton turned and looked at the kids. "You are all winners in my book. I know that fame and rewards are not the reasons you do what you do. But

I do want to show my appreciation in some small way. Therefore, the runners-up will have their names engraved on a brick that will line the entryway to the park. They will also receive a $100 dollar gift certificate to Mr. Douglas's toy store."

Applause and a few cheers.

"But the grand prize winner of the first ever Hamilton Park Award will receive their name on a plaque that will be placed on a memorial in the middle of the square...*and* an all-access pass to the rides, attractions, shows, and treats of Hamilton Park for the whole season."

The crowd oohed and aahed.

Felix nearly fell out of his seat. He steadied himself and said to his friends, "I knew about the toy store cash and the general honor of the thing, but season passes to Hamilton Park—think of all the deep fat fried things, all the concerts, all the Creepy time."

Mr. Hamilton continued. "To introduce the nominees, I have behind me a gentleman who knows them well. Of course, I am speaking about the Principal of Ravensburg Middle School, Dr. Cooling."

Principal Cooling came to the mic. "Thank you, thank you, thank you. But I know you didn't come here today to listen to me, so let me introduce the nominees for the first ever Hamilton Park Award. Kids, please stand as I call your names. First, we have The Rollerblader's Against Littering. They combine an obsession for exercise with a passion for a cleaner Ravensburg."

The crowd cheered and four kids wearing knee pads and helmets rolled in circles high-fiving each other.

"Our second group is Up A Tree. These kids spend their afternoons and weekends rescuing marooned cats and kittens, allowing the Ravensburg Fire Department to focus on its less furry citizens."

More cheering. Three very tall kids stood up and bowed in half at the applause.

"Our third group goes by many names, but they are on this stage today because of their work as Students Against Split Infinitives. They've turned their hatred of all things ungrammatical into a flourishing elementary school enhancement program."

The English Club stood up and waved at the crowd: elbow, elbow, wrist, wrist.

"And our fourth group," said Principal Cooling, "is well known to all Ravensburg, and has received not a little notoriety for quick thinking and bravery. They have even helped our very own police department solve several important cases. Of course, I'm speaking of none other than....the MATH INSPECTORS!"

The loudest cheers yet greeted the Math Inspectors as they rose. Stanley nodded, the girls waved, Herman looked at the ground and flushed a little, and Felix grasped both hands above his head and shook them like a conquering hero.

"As Mr. Hamilton said," continued Principal Cooling, "you are all to be commended for your service. And now, the moment we've all been waiting for..." Principal Cooling picked up a golden envelope on the podium, and opened it. The crowd hushed.

"The first winner of the Hamilton Park Awards is—"

"The MATH INSPECTORS!" blared a voice over the speaker system.

The Math Inspectors jumped up in excitement. The rollerbladers and cat rescuers congratulated them. It was only when they turned towards the podium that they first noticed a problem.

Not a single person in the crowd was clapping. Most of the people seemed confused, and some of them were murmuring.

"Good day, good people of Ravensburg," blared the voice on the loudspeaker. "For the purpose of today's exercise, you may call me MacBeth."

The voice was obviously not coming from either man at the podium, who stood staring at each other in confusion. Stanley looked around the square to find someone else with a mic, but didn't see anyone. Then he noticed some people in the crowd pointing at the jumbo screen behind the stage. Stanley snapped his eyes to it. A huge yellow smiley face looked down at them. Its black eyes darted back and forth, as if it was looking for something. Underneath the face was written the word *MacBeth*. The friends climbed up for a better look.

The smiley face opened its mouth and spoke. "No time to twaddle. Shall we begin?"

Stanley was starting to dislike something about the voice. It sounded neither male nor female. It was high-pitched yet melodic. In fact, it was hard to determine anything distinguishing about it. That wasn't what bothered him, though. It had an edge to it. Something unpleasant. Something like sarcasm.

"Watch carefully, now," it said.

The big screen snapped to a split view. On the left was the smiley face. But now on the right there were two boxes, one on top of the other. Each contained a streaming image. The image on top was of the podium. The bottom one was a video feed of something else.

"The Hamilton Roller Coaster," several voices shouted at once.

"If you look carefully," said the smiley face, "you will notice that these are live images. And yes, that is a close up of the first drop of the Hamilton Roller Coaster. *Your* beloved Hamilton Roller Coaster."

Stanley made up his mind: he did not like the voice.

Dr. Cooling looked at Mr. Hamilton, who seemed just as confused as everyone else. The principal leaned over and spoke sideways into the mic so he could see the video screen. "Who are you?" he asked.

"Tut, tut, tut," said MacBeth. "It sounds like somebody left his listening ears at home today. Hopefully the students are paying better attention than their principal. But now would be a good time to start paying attention, dear Dr. Cooling, because there is something I need you to do. I need you to contact the Ravensburg Police Department and inform them about the bombs attached to the first drop of the Hamilton Roller Coaster. Three very large, very powerful bombs they are; the kind of bombs that will reduce that roller coaster to sawdust."

CHAPTER THREE

RULES OF THE GAME

"No!" screamed Mr. Hamilton.

"What do you mean bombs?" Principal Cooling said. "Is this some kind of twisted joke?"

MacBeth smiled. "Twisted? Hmm, maybe it is. But a joke it most definitely is not. Think of it as an educational exercise. In a way, you should thank me. Principals are always trying to find ways to make things educational, right?"

"Educational?" Dr. Cooling blared. "How in the world is this educational?"

"Simple," said MacBeth. "Think of it as word problem with real world applications. Write this down if you need to: There are three large bombs attached to the Hamilton Roller Coaster. They are set to detonate at 3 pm today. If the key to disarming the bombs can be won in a game, which brave souls will risk it all to save a National Landmark?"

The crowd began to stir.

"Call the police, Dr. Cooling," MacBeth said. "They may hesitate to believe you, and that is why the same video image you are enjoying can also be accessed on my new website: *BlowingUpHamiltonRollerCoaster.com*. Please direct the police to that website so they can examine the bombs from a distance and verify my claims."

"This is outrageous," said Mr. Hamilton. "This is my park, and I'm not about to play along with your sick game."

MacBeth looked solemn. "Luckily for the town of Ravensburg, then, you are not on my list of contestants. And that leads me to Rule Number One: Only a chosen few people may participate in our present proceedings. The lucky players are, in fact, some of Ravensburg's most prized students, a group that calls itself the Math Inspectors. You know who you are, Math Inspectors, and I know who you are, so why not come up to the podium and speak for yourselves?"

Felix, Charlotte, Gertie, and Herman turned to Stanley, but none of them moved.

MacBeth's eyes beamed down at them. "Why be bashful now, Math Inspectors? You certainly have not minded the spotlight these past few months. Step up. Step up, and be recognized."

Stanley stared into MacBeth's face and hesitated. Then he slowly walked to the podium and the others followed. They turned and faced the screen and saw themselves in the top box.

MacBeth nodded. "Wave to all the people who are watching you on *BlowingUpHamiltonRollerCoaster.com*. My website has suddenly... exploded with traffic."

"What do you want?" asked Gertie into the mic.

"All business, eh Gertrude? I have always liked that about you. And you have a point, the clock is ticking. Let me bottom line this for you—I want you to solve a series of riddles, find the key that will diffuse the bombs, and save the day. Or at least, I want you to try."

"I think you're bluffing," said Gertie. "And so does Felix."

Felix turned red. "I don't know if I'd say bluffing.

Joking, perhaps. I mean, you do smile a lot."

MacBeth's smile seemed to grow larger. "Bluffing, you say? Well, not everyone thinks so. Charlotte has already made up her mind that I am not bluffing, but a lot of other people are still undecided. So let me assure you, those bombs are real. And if you do not play by the rules, that roller coaster will be gone in the blink of an eye."

Gertie put her hands on her hips. "It's just a little hard to believe that the person behind such a totally cute smiley face is an evil genius that blows stuff up. We're just supposed to take your word for it?"

"Not at all," said MacBeth. "You know how writers try to avoid *telling* whenever possible? That is because good writers are supposed to *show,* not tell. And do you know why? Because telling is so boring. Let me prove it with a little show of my own."

Stanley saw the flash of the fireball a split second before he felt its concussive force. Even though he was fifty yards from the explosion, he covered his head instinctively. When he looked up there was lots of yelling and screaming. Something in the park was on fire.

"Watch out!" screamed one of the tall kids from Up A Tree.

Just then something came falling from the sky, a flaming red ball of some kind. It landed in the middle of the stage and rolled, screeching, "Ha, ha, Haaaaaaaa!" And then it said no more.

It was none other than the blown off head from the Creepy the Clown ride.

"Noooo!" screamed Felix. "Creeeeeepyyyyy!"

"Did you just scream in slow motion?" asked Gertie.

"He just killed Creepy!" yelled Felix. "MacBeth blew him sky high!"

Stanley looked at the billowing smoke and then to Charlotte for confirmation.

Charlotte shrugged. "If you need more than the clown nose's death cry," she said, pointing at the red ball short-circuiting in front of them, "then yes, that's exactly where the ride is. Or was."

"As least we know nobody was anywhere near it," said Herman. "But this guy really means business."

Felix sobbed. The crowd screamed. And Stanley grabbed the mic.

"What do we have to do?"Stanley said.

Every person in the park seemed to hear Stanley's voice at the same time, because they all quieted immediately and turned to the big screen.

MacBeth broke into a menacing laugh. "The game is afoot, then? Wonderful. Here are the rules to live by:

"One: Only the Math Inspectors may play. If anyone else attempts to solve the riddles—the bombs will detonate.

"Two: Math Inspectors, you must find the key to deactivate the bombs. If you fail to accomplish this by 3pm—the bombs will detonate.

"Three: If anyone else goes near the Hamilton Roller Coaster—the bombs will detonate. Any questions?"

"I have one," said Principal Cooling. "What makes you think we're going to stand by while you do this to these kids?"

"Do what?" MacBeth looked insulted. "I am not making them do anything. Math Inspectors, hear me clearly: you are under no obligation to participate. You may choose right now to sit quietly by until time expires, at which time you may watch the fireworks display from the comfort and safety of the parking lot with the rest of the crowd. You may also decide at any moment today that you have had enough, at which time you may walk away from the whole thing. No one will blame you. But as long as you continue to solve the case...well, as long as you do that, I cannot guarantee either your comfort or your safety. What do you say, Math Inspectors? Will you sit by and let things run their course? Or will you walk out the front gates and see what adventures await?"

Stanley knew all eyes were on him. He looked at the screen. But then his gaze focused just beyond it to the top of the Hamilton Roller Coaster. It stood where it had for over a century, its wooden scaffolding, its steep climbs, and its massive drops now silent, like everything else in the park, as if it too was waiting for his answer.

Stanley slowly pushed his glasses to his face, took a step forward, and looked directly into the screen. "We're in."

CHAPTER FOUR

OPERATION INTERFERENCE

"Oh, good," squealed MacBeth. "Shall we begin? I hate waiting. The five of you will be allowed to leave immediately and go anywhere you like. All that you have to do is find the key to diffuse the bomb. The clock begins ticking now."

Two things happened at once on the screen. A red light started blinking on a box attached to the bombs, and a clue replaced MacBeth's name on the screen. It read:

The distance from Here to where you belong
Is the precise hypotenuse of Camp's oblong.

Stanley snapped into action without turning away from MacBeth. "Charlotte?" he said.

"Done," she tapped the side of her head.

"Gertie?" Stanley asked.

"Already have it written down," she said.

"And not just the words—copy it exactly," said Stanley.

"Right."

"Felix?"

"What do you want me to do? The crazy floating head hasn't exactly offered us hors d'oeuvres."

"Fair enough."

Stanley crossed the stage towards the stairs, and his friends followed. He checked his watch. They had about six hours to find the key and diffuse the bombs. He turned around and looked at MacBeth again. The face smiled and winked. Then he turned to Mr. Hamilton and said, "We're going to find that key." The old man tried to speak but couldn't.

Dr. Cooling took out his cell phone. "And I'm going to do what he asked and call the police. I think Chief Abrams will have something to say about your playing this crazy game."

The kids walked down the stairs and another path opened in front of them, this time leading away from the stage. People stared at them as they passed, but while some smiled weakly, nobody said a thing. Just as they left the square, the friends heard MacBeth's voice one last time. "Ta ta for now, Math Inspectors. I do hope you enjoy my little treasure hunt. We are going to have such a blast today."

Stanley positively hated that voice.

After making their way to the park exit, the friends were mobbed by a team of police officers with Chief Abrams at their head. Several other people crowded around, too.

Everyone was talking at once, but Chief Abrams took the kids aside. "Someone in the crowd called us already. We heard the whole thing. Sounds like we've got a real nut job on our hands. I've called in the bomb squad. If you kids are up to it, I need you to run interference."

"What do you mean by *interference*?" Stanley asked.

Abrams barked an order into his walkie-talkie, then turned to Stanley. "Look, all I need is for you five kids to keep this MacBeth guy busy by playing his little games as long as you can. We have protocols and training to deal with situations like this, and we're already working every angle we can think of. Of course, there is no way of knowing exactly what criminals like this will do, but we've been given a break here and I intend to use it."

"A break?" Charlotte said. "You mean us?"

"That's exactly what I mean," said the chief. "For some reason, MacCrazy is interested in you Math Inspectors. If it was just money he was after, he could have contacted us directly. But this guy wants to drag the process out and dangle a little hope in front of our faces with riddles. We can use that against him."

"But, Chief," began Stanley, "you have to give us a chance—"

"No, Stanley," Abrams held up a hand to cut him off. "There is no way I'm going to let you try to actually solve this thing. I need you to play along for a little while, that's all."

Stanley's phone rang. He sighed. "It's my mom. Something tells me convincing you is nothing compared to convincing her."

The other kids' phones were ringing, too. Several

minutes later they all hung up.

"Well?" asked Abrams.

"Well," said Stanley. "At first my parents were set against me doing anything other than staying home for the next twenty years or so. But then they agreed with you that we could be useful as long as we stayed out of danger."

The others nodded.

"My parents added a proviso," said Gertie. "They said I can't step one foot out of the park without being under the supervision of my favorite resource officer and yours, Officer Evans."

The chief leaned into his walkie-talkie. "Evans, I need you at the front of Hamilton Park with your cruiser." He turned to Stanley. "Evans will have eyes on you the whole time. Do what you need to do to play this twisted scavenger hunt, but your objective is NOT to find that key. Your objective is to keep MacBeth's attention elsewhere so we can figure out how to disarm those bombs. Are we clear?"

"But we—"

"Are we clear?"

"Crystal," said Stanley.

Chief Abrams put a hand on Stanley's shoulder. "Not that you've ever listened to me before, but this time I really do mean it, let the professionals handle this. Don't underestimate how dangerous this MacBeth is. Stay safe."

Stanley nodded.

Abrams was on his radio again. He walked back to the crowd of people and began giving orders. The kids were alone at the drop off zone in front of the park.

Stanley turned to his friends. "I don't care what

he says. We can do this, guys."

Felix folded his long arms. "Yeah, sure. Bombs, deranged happy faces, ticking clocks. We do this stuff all the time."

Gertie shoved a pencil behind her ear and pocketed her notepad. "These next words feel really weird in my head, so I can only imagine how strange they are going to sound when I say them out loud, but... I agree with Chief Abrams, Stanley. We should let the professionals handle this. Yep, that definitely felt weird."

Stanley looked at Charlotte. "Is that what you think, too?"

Charlotte looked at him for a moment without responding. "I don't like it," she said. "It's too dangerous."

"What do you mean?" said Stanley. "We've been up against bad guys before. You were the one who wouldn't give up when we were after the Grinch. And that guy was a creep."

Charlotte shook her head. "No. This is different. The Grinch was out for money. This guy is out for something else. Stanley, this guy just blew up an amusement park ride."

"Let's be honest," interrupted Gertie. "The demise of Creepy the Clown was more like a public service."

Felix sniffled.

"Either way," continued Charlotte, "this guy means business. And he's come after us specifically. Doesn't that freak you out?"

"No," said Stanley, "that's actually what makes me believe we can do this."

His friends all stared at him.

"Don't you see?" he explained. "This MacBeth guy picked *us* out to solve the riddles. It only follows logic that they are problems we are capable of solving."

"Wow," said Gertie, "that makes about as much sense as Felix on a kale and spinach diet."

Felix perked up a little. "Would the kale and spinach be in the form of ice cream?" he asked. "Because if we're talking a mint-oreo-kale-and-spinach smoothie, then Stanley might be making more sense than I first thought."

Stanley turned to Herman. "Do you think this

whole thing is a lost cause, too?"

Herman shoved his hands into his baggy short pockets and looked down for a moment. "Maybe. Of course, we won't know until we try. And I'm in favor of trying. But I *am* kinda weird."

"Well obviously we all agree with that," said Gertie. "First that Herman is a little weird. But also, *of course* we should give it a try. I never said we should give up before we start. I just wanted to be on record as saying 'This is not going to work!' so I get to rub it in later."

"You're going to do a Gertie victory dance when tiny little specks of roller coaster dust settle upon the streets of Ravensburg?" said Felix.

Gertie frowned at him. "I, of course, would wait for a better time to rub it in. But yes, you get the general idea. So with that in mind, I'm in."

"Well," said Felix, "I intend to avenge my dear ol' pal, Creepy. I'm in, too."

Stanley looked at Charlotte. "Well?"

She crossed her arms and looked at him for a whole minute before answering. "Okay, we'll work the first clue. There's a lot of sense in what the chief says, anyway. If we can occupy MacBeth's attention, the cops can do their job more effectively. But I'm telling you right now, Stanley Carusoe, at the first sign of real danger I'm pulling the plug."

Stanley smiled. "Then let's work the first clue."

CHAPTER FIVE

HISTORY CLASS TO THE RESCUE

Gertie retrieved her notepad and handed it to Stanley. He reread the first clue aloud.

The distance from Here to where you belong
Is the precise hypotenuse of Camp's oblong.

"Charlotte, anything interesting?"

She squinted. "MacBeth capitalized *Here* and *Camp's*. A guy like this probably doesn't do anything by mistake, so there's a reason those two words are capitalized."

"Good. Felix, how about you?"

"Hypotenuse: the longest side of a right triangle. Except in this clue it says the hypotenuse of an oblong."

Gertie jumped in. "Yeah, that's weird. Oblong is something that's longer than it is wide. So, normally that would refer to a rectangle not a triangle, right?"

"That's right." Stanley agreed. "Oblong usually refers to a rectangle. But who is Camp? And why is his or her rectangle so important?"

Felix thumbed his phone to life. "Searching famous people with the last name Camp. Okay, I have about thirty million results."

"Cross reference that with rectangle," said Stanley.

"Got it. Come here and see if any of this jumps out at you."

They all gathered around the phone.

"Well," Stanley said, "I don't think I know any of these. The only one that remotely rings a bell is Walter Camp."

"Me too," said Gertie.

Felix clicked on Walter Camp's name and read: "A football player and coach. Known as the Father of American Football."

Stanley hit the side of his head. "Of course. Coach Bellum's World History class last year, remember?"

Gertie smirked. "You mean Coach Bellum's Football History class, right? Wow, do you know what this means? It means we actually learned something in that class. And it also means one of us remembered something Charlotte's photographic memory did not."

Charlotte smiled. "Eidetic memory, actually. But I have to be paying attention for it to work. Which didn't happen much in that class."

"Good point," said Gertie. "Nobody but Stanley paid any attention."

"Be glad I did," said Stanley. "Okay, Camp's oblong means Walter Camp's rectangle. So, the Father of American Football's most famous rectangle would be?"

"A football field," said Charlotte.

Stanley nodded. "Felix, the exact dimensions of a football field."

"Right. Here it is. From endzone to endzone, it's 100 yards, which is 300 feet. From sideline to sideline, it's 53.33 yards, which is 160 feet."

"Now we're getting somewhere," Stanley said. "Gertie, hand your notebook to Herman so he can sketch a rectangular football field to scale and label the distances."

After Herman was done, they all looked over his shoulder.

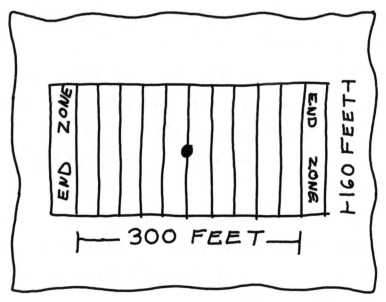

"But we still have a problem," Gertie pointed out. "How do we find the hypotenuse of a rectangle?"

"Like this," said Stanley. He grabbed Gertie's pencil and drew a line from the corner of one endzone to the opposite corner of the other endzone, splitting the football field into two large triangles.

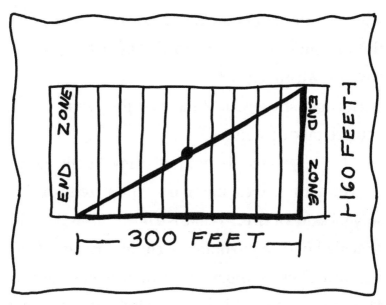

"That's got to be it," said Felix. "So one leg of our new triangle has a length of 160 feet, and the other leg of our triangle has a length of 300 feet. In order to find the hypotenuse of that triangle, we use the Pythagorean theorem: $a^2 + b = c^2$."

"Or, in this case," Gertie said, "160 squared plus 300 squared = the hypotenuse squared."

"Right," said Felix, "160 ft squared plus 300 ft squared is 115,600 ft squared. Then we take the square root of that and are left with..." Felix did the calculations in his head and smiled. "340 feet. That's our hypotenuse."

Stanley flipped the notebook back and forth

studying the clue and the diagram. "Okay, then the distance from *Here* to the next clue is 340 feet. Do we all agree?"

Herman shrugged. "I have no idea what any of you are talking about."

"I think 340 feet is right, Stanley," Felix said.

"That still leaves one more capitalized word to solve," said Gertie. "What is *Here*? Oh wait," she squealed before anyone else could answer. "*Here Today & Gone Tomorrow*. It's a little boutique on Main Street that sells beauty products. I'm there all the time. I bet that's it."

Just then Officer Evan's drove up in his cruiser. They jumped in.

"Sorry it took so long," the young officer said. "I was across town when I got the call. Where to?" Having seen the Math Inspectors in action, Evans wasn't about to ask for the why's and how's. They had, after all, helped him solve several cases over the last year.

"Main Street," said Stanley. Evans nodded and turned on his flashing lights. Within ten minutes they were on the cobblestone streets of downtown Ravensburg.

Evans leaned an arm out of his open window. "What can I do to help?"

Stanley thought for a moment, then shook his head. "MacBeth's first rule stated that we are the only ones allowed to figure a way out of this mess. Giving us a ride is one thing, but helping us puzzle out this problem is another. We'd better not risk this maniac blowing his top. If you don't mind, the best thing you can do is stay in your car and listen to any developments on the radio."

Evans nodded. "As long as I can keep two eyes on you five. Those are my orders."

The friends gathered at the front of *Here Today & Gone Tomorrow,* and Gertie reread her notes. "So, 340 feet from *Here* is our next clue."

"You wouldn't happen to have a measuring tape in those handy pockets of yours, would you, Herman?" asked Felix.

"Nope. Left the measuring tape in my other cargo pants. I do have a carpenter's level and an electric toothbrush in these, if that helps."

"You still scare me, you know that right?" said Felix.

"We don't need a tape measure." Herman pointed down. "How long do you think these bricks are?"

"Six inches," Charlotte said with certainty.

"Good point, Herman," said Stanley. "From the front door of the store, we need to go 680 bricks until we hit the next clue. But there's nothing in the clue about which direction to go."

Gertie shrugged. "Then we all pick a different direction and see where we end up."

The kids started at the front door of the boutique and fanned out slowly, counting bricks down Main Street. Stanley and Charlotte ended up at different points in the middle of the street.

"Nothing here," said Charlotte. "Stones are solid. No manholes leading to the sewers. Nothing written anywhere."

"Same here," said Stanley. "Anything, Felix?"

Felix's count had taken him across Main Street and straight to Mabel's Diner. "Oh baby. I've got something big here, guys. From where I'm standing, I can just make out today's lunch special. All-you-can-eat fish and chips. Upgrade to endless baked beans for 99 cents more. How does she make enough money to stay open with those prices?"

"Felix, if you upgrade to endless baked beans, you'll need to downgrade to different friends," said

Gertie. "Now do you see anything clue-ish over there or not?"

"You can sure suck the fun out of a death-defying scavenger hunt, you know that, Short Stuff?" said Felix. "No, I got nothing here."

"Me neither," said Gertie, standing on the sidewalk outside an empty storefront. "No lights on at Franklin's Jewelry Store these days. Herman's spot looks more promising, anyway. I'm headed his way."

Herman stood a few feet from a large fountain in the middle of Main Street's only roundabout. The other four joined him.

"Are you standing on brick 680?" Stanley asked.

"I'm at 642," said Herman. "Which means I've got almost another twenty feet to go. Problem is," he pointed at the fountain, "this is in the way."

Stanley looked at the fountain for a moment and wondered why, as many times as he'd passed by it, he'd never examined it closely before. In the middle, stood a large statue of a World War I soldier holding his rifle in the air and screaming. Water sprayed out of small fountains shaped like canons mounted on the short stone walls surrounding the statue. The pool was filled to a depth of about two feet.

Charlotte hopped onto the wall. "I don't think that's a problem. Twenty feet puts you in the pool. It would be a good place to hide something."

She hopped into the water. The others followed, and for several minutes they poked around into every crevice they could find. Nothing.

Suddenly, Charlotte froze and looked up into the statue's face. Then she motioned to Herman and boosted him up on top of the figure's shoulders.

Herman nodded. "There's something here in the statue's mouth. Looks like a piece of paper." He grabbed it out and unfolded it. "Yep, this is it. Clue #2."

CHAPTER SIX

SQUARES AND ALIENS

The Math Inspectors sat on two long benches in front of the fountain, dripping wet but smiling. They'd found the second clue.

Charlotte read it aloud.

Congratulations, Math Inspectors. I am clue #2.

My name is $x2 + y2 + 4x - 6y + 11 = 0$.

Stanley, who can complete me but you?

Stanley took the paper. "That looks like the long form of the equation of a circle, right?"

Felix, Gertie, and Charlotte nodded.

Stanley continued. "Meaning this has something to do with a circle defined by that equation?"

Felix shook his head. "Yeah, but you know better

than anybody that it's not really useful until we put that equation in a different form. And to do that we need to—"

Stanley put his head in his hands. "Complete the square. MacBeth wants us to complete the square on this equation. That's impossible." Stanley loved math. And he was great at math. Most of the time. The one problem he consistently messed up was completing the square.

Charlotte took the note. "We can figure this out."

"It's not just that," said Stanley. "How could MacBeth know that *I* struggle with completing the square problems?"

Charlotte answered without hesitation. "I don't know, but I know exactly why he's doing it. Stanley, he's trying to ruffle your feathers, get under your skin. You gotta shake it off and just focus on the problem."

"It just doesn't make—"

"Stanley! Focus. On. The. Problem."

"You're right. You're right. But I'm not doing it. The first answer to this riddle is that anybody but me can complete the square."

"Not true," said Herman. "All those numbers look like what happens when gobblygook gives birth to gibberish to me."

Stanley smiled slightly. "Felix, you want to do the honors?"

Felix was the completing-the-square champion of the group, and he never let the others forget it.

"Step aside, Halflings. Uncle Felix is here to save the day." Felix wrote down the long form of the equation. "Okay, the first step is to get the constant number onto the other side of the equation." He subtracted 11 from both sides. "Then, we group the x's together and the y's together." He showed them his work.

$$x^2 + 4x + y^2 - 6y = -11$$

He put the pen behind his ears and cracked his knuckles. "Okay, now is the tricky part. If you're a three-year-old, maybe. Oh, sorry Stanley. What I mean is, *this* is where the magic happens."

"And this is the part I can never get past," said Stanley. "It's a mental block or something."

Felix looked at him. "Just think of it this way. Imagine that we take x2 + 4x and try to turn it into a perfect square. To do that we take half of 4, which is 2. Then we square 2 and that gives us 4. So our new polynomial is $x2 + 4x + 4$. We do the same thing to the y's. We take half of $-6y$ which is -3 and then square it, and that gives us 9. So our new polynomial is $y2 - 6y + 9$. Rewriting everything together, we get this." He turned his notes around.

$$(x2 + 4x + 4) + (y2 - 6x + 9) = -11$$

"Easy," said Felix.

"Yeah. Super easy," said Herman dryly.

"Of course, I know what you're all thinking. The problem is that, as it stands, we currently have 13 more on the left side than when we started the problem, so we have to add 13 to the right side as well to keep everything balanced. Final step, we are going to rewrite these polynomials in their perfect square form. And obviously you see what you're left with."

$$(x + 2) 2 + (y - 3) 2 = 2$$

"Obviously," said Herman. "I'm thinking about going back to a life of crime."

Gertie snatched her notepad back. "Which means $x = -2$ and $y = 3$. So this equation describes a circle that can be found at the point (−2,3) with the radius of 2."

"Nicely done, Felix," said Stanley. "So the clue is a circle with a center at the point (−2,3) and with a radius of 2. But (−2,3) what? And from where? What's our coordinate plane?"

Felix scratched his chin thoughtfully. "It's gotta be the town."

"Okay then," said Stanley, "let's say our starting point is right here at the fountain where we found clue #2. What is 2 miles west and 3 miles north of here? Anything interesting?"

"That's right about where the Adirondack Forest starts to get really thick," answered Charlotte. "I've hunted there lots of times."

Felix brought up his map app, marked their current spot, and scrolled over 2 miles west and 3 miles north. He placed a red x at that location. "Charlotte's right, the forest really starts to thicken up just north of there, but at the exact spot of the coordinates is an open field."

Charlotte looked carefully at Felix's screen and her eyes widened. "That's Farmer Dahlgren's land.

Okay, I get it. There is one very unique thing about his fields. Felix, zoom in." As he did the map closed in on a hole the size of a house. They looked at Charlotte for an explanation. "That's the crater left behind from a meteorite that hit Mr. Dahlgren's farmland decades ago."

Stanley looked at his watch. It was 10:30. "What do you bet MacBeth placed our next clue at the middle of that crater? Let's get going." They jumped in Officer Evan's cruiser, he turned on his siren, and off they went.

"Anything from the chief?" Stanley said.

"No," said Evans. "At least, nothing he could say over the radio."

Fifteen minutes later, they'd made it through the back roads to Farmer Dahlgren's place. He was in the barn feeding the pigs.

"Hello, Mr. Dahlgren," said Charlotte.

"Well hello, Charlotte. Hunting again today?"

"Sort of," said Charlotte. "But not the usual kind."

Evans broke in. "We have a situation here that involves your farm, sir. Do you mind if the kids and

I took a look at that crater?"

The old farmer grinned. "It's the aliens you're here for, isn't it?"

"Aliens?" said Evans.

"I knew someday somebody would be coming about the aliens," said the old farmer, wiping his hands on his overalls. "I knew ever since the day my grandpappy took me out there when it was still smoking and says: 'Lambert, someday somebody is gonna be coming about the aliens that caused this here crater.' And now finally, here you are."

"We're not here because of something crazy like aliens," said Gertie. "We're here because a giant floating head told us to come here and look for Clue #3."

"Right," said Dahlgren with a wink. He pointed up. "Better not talk about *them* in the open. I read you loud and clear, missy. But if you want to see the crater, you're going to need to take my truck. Trails out to the field are a little long to walk and a little rough for a police car."

Evans looked hesitantly at the ancient pickup truck, but Stanley motioned to his watch. Evans swung the passenger door open while the kids piled into the bed of the truck.

For several minutes they all held on for dear life as Dahlgren tore through his fields. "It's coming up," said Charlotte. "I know this area pretty well. We got permission years ago from Mr. Dahlgren to pass through his place to get to the woods. Dad's brought me out here to see the crater lots of times."

Farmer Dahlgren parked at the edge of the enormous hole and grabbed a shotgun from the three mounted on the back of the truck's cab. "Not sure if bullets will work on them," he nodded upward. "But I'm more than willing to find out. You kids do what you need to. I'll cover you."

The kids scrambled down to the center of the crater and noticed a rock sat at a funny angle. Under it was a small silver and black box. Felix grabbed the box and flipped the top open slowly, worried that something unpleasant was set to fly out.

But the box only contained a cell phone. When Felix hit the power button, a text message popped up.

Remember the rule about solving this alone? You're pressing your luck.

"You have to show him," said Charlotte.

The kids climbed out of the crater and Stanley held the phone up to Evans.

Evans scanned the perimeter quickly. "That means MacBeth can see us. He has to be close by." Evans grabbed his radio and pushed down the call button, but before he could get a word out, a piercing noise made the kids shut their ears in pain. It finally stopped and Evans pushed buttons and turned knobs in vain.

"My radio's been jammed," Evans said. He took out his phone. "Cell phone won't work either."

Farmer Dahlgren cocked his gun, balanced it on the hood of the truck, and looked through the sights up into the clear blue sky. "They'll be coming from that way when they come, the aliens."

"Were there really aliens that landed on your farm?" asked Felix.

"How else do you explain the enormous hole in front of you?" said the farmer.

Gertie pointed at the crater. "It's called a meteorite. A big cosmic rock landed here. There is absolutely no evidence that aliens exist. As much as I wish there was."

Dahlgren chuckled and continued to scan the sky. "No evidence, huh? I'll tell you something, little lady, there is no evidence that meteorites exist either."

"Scientists track them all the time through telescopes," said Gertie.

The old farmer spit. "So they claim. I don't trust scientists, and I've never seen a meteorite with my own eyes. But aliens, well, look at this big crater here. What more proof do you need?"

"Wow," said Felix. "When I grow up, Farmer Dahlgren, I want to be a harmless old coot, just like you."

"Thank you, son," said Dahlgren. "Now grab a shotgun out of the pickup and stand with me against annihilation."

Felix ran towards the pickup, but Evans grabbed him by his collar and held him back. "What I really need right now is a landline phone. Do you have one back at the house, Mr. Dahlgren?"

"Still got the old rotary phone bolted to the wall, just for such an occasion. You kids get in the truck and I'll cover you."

"Let's go," Evans said.

"But the text message says for you and Mr. Dahlgren to leave," said Stanley. "I think we are supposed to stay."

"How many times do I have to say this?" said Evans. "There is zero chance I'm letting you kids out of my sight today. Now get back in the truck!"

Gertie turned to Stanley when they were halfway back to the farmhouse. "I don't get it. We found the phone, but the message didn't sound like a clue. It was more like a threat. What are we supposed to do now?"

Stanley looked at Charlotte. "I don't think you're going to like this, but—" just then the phone in Stanley's hand buzzed. He read the message on the screen:

You know what you need to do. Now do it!

CHAPTER SEVEN

STRANGE MATH

"No," said Charlotte. "Absolutely not. We are not ditching Officer Evans."

"But Charlotte," said Stanley, "you know as well as I do that we aren't going to get another clue while Evans is around. I'm not saying we do anything dangerous. I'm just saying we go out on our own long enough to figure out what Clue #3 is."

"We're not even discussing this," said Charlotte.

When they reached the farmhouse, Farmer Dahlgren pulled into the barn and shut off his old truck. "This way to the phone," he said.

Evans followed him to the small whitewashed farmhouse. "You kids head to my cruiser. I'm going to check in with the chief."

When the door of the farmhouse banged shut Stanley turned to his friends. "This is our last chance. Once we get back to the station, they're not going to let us out again till it's too late."

Nobody said anything.

"Let's at least get the next clue," Stanley pleaded. "We can still pull the plug if we think it's crazy."

"This whole thing is crazy," said Gertie.

"What do you think is going to happen if we stop playing along?" said Stanley. "Game over. Do you want to be responsible for a National Landmark going up in flames on your watch?"

The phone buzzed.

Stanley froze. Then he looked down and smiled. "It seems we're far enough away from Evans to get the next clue after all. Listen to this."

Clue #3:
A common pair of 1 and 8
Awaits discovery in the wood.
But its true meaning lies on a table
Where 18 x 7 does not equal what it should.

"Say what?" said Herman.

Felix sighed. "Either I'm stupid or these are getting harder."

"You're stupid about lots of stuff," said Gertie.

"But not math. These *are* getting harder, and I don't have a clue what that clue means."

Charlotte stood up and looked at the tree line not far from the farmhouse. "I don't either, but the answer is somewhere out there."

Stanley stood next to her. "Tell us what you can about it, Charlotte."

"Well, like I said before, this is where the Adirondacks get hard to travel. There are trails, but for the most part the forest is thick and dense."

Gertie bounced up on her tippy toes. "Looks woody. And dark. Are there many large, girl-eating animals in there?"

"A few," said Charlotte.

Gertie folded her arms. "Sounds like a terrific place to build a summer home."

"At least," said Felix, searching the sky, "that thick canopy of trees is pretty good cover from the aliens."

"Oh for goodness sake," snapped Gertie. "For the last time, Felix, there are no such thing as—"

Just then they heard voices coming from the farmhouse.

Stanley turned and faced his friends. "Decision time. I still think we can do this. What do you say?"

Herman nodded. "I'm in."

Felix gave a thumbs up. "Me too."

Gertie shook her head. "I'd love to reenact *The Wizard of Oz* with you, Stanley, but even Charlotte doesn't think we should go into the woods."

"Actually," said Charlotte. "I think that forest is one of the few places I'd feel comfortable taking us. I know it like the back of my hand. What's more, I know lots of hiding places, and we'd be harder to track. It's an ideal place for Operation Diversion. As long as I can keep an eye on the rest of you, I'm in."

"Then let's move," said Stanley.

Charlotte took off towards the tree line and plunged into the woods. The others followed. They turned around just in time to see Evans coming out of the farmhouse. He ran into the barn and called their names.

"I feel bad about that," said Herman. "As cops go, Evans is a nice guy."

"Can't be helped," said Stanley. "But I don't like it, either."

"He'll get over it," said Gertie. "But boy, I would not want to be him when he breaks the news to my parents."

"It won't take him long before he checks here," said Charlotte. "We'd better start walking as we work the problem."

Stanley reread Clue #3 and asked for ideas.

"The common pair of 1 and 8," Felix offered, "would give us the number 18, or the number 81, or 9, or 7."

"So what do we do with that information?" asked Gertie.

"The clue says their meaning would be revealed in a table," said Stanley. "Charlotte, are there cabins in this part of the Adirondacks?"

"I don't think so. Most of this beyond Dahlgren's is federal land, so no private cabins. There are some park ranger outposts that watch for forest fires. Could that be it?"

"I don't know." Stanley checked his watch. This was taking too much time. "Maybe it's a big hunk of rock or stone that looks like a table. But what was the part about 18 x 7 not equaling what it should?

Felix, what should 18 x 7 equal?"

"126."

Stanley frowned. "So whatever this table is, it shows us that 18 x 7 does not equal 126. And somehow this table reveals to us the true meaning of this common pairing of 1 and 8."

They walked in silence for some time.

Suddenly, Felix snapped his fingers. "Maybe it's the dimensions of a picnic table. Ever see any around here?"

Charlotte shook her head. "Nope. This area isn't exactly the family picnic type. At least none of the parts I've hiked."

Gertie rubbed her head as if massaging her brain. "I think I'm more confused now." She sat down on a fallen tree. "It's time for a break. And with all this picnic talk I'm as starving as a six-foot, red-headed kid at a funnel-cake-eating contest. Anybody bring a snack?"

Charlotte was carrying a small black sports bag. She slung it off now and loosened the strings binding the main compartment. They all sat down and watched as pretzels, sandwiches, fruit, and canteens of water appeared.

"Why all the emergency supplies?" Stanley teased.

"They weren't my idea," Charlotte laughed. "I was supposed to go straight from the park to Gertie's today, and my dad always loads me up with goodies for slumber parties. Says it's 'just good manners' to bring something with." She tossed a Jell-O cup to Felix.

"A great man, your father," said Felix. He opened the Jell-O and squeezed the whole thing into his mouth.

"Well," said Stanley, "there's probably no reason to move from here until we know which way to go. Thoughts?"

The only reply was chomping and smacking from the kids and an occasional snap or creak from the trees around them.

After a while, Charlotte bent down and studied some deer tracks at her feet. "When my dad takes me hunting, sometimes the trail gets confusing. The more confusing it gets, dad tells me to go with the trail that's the most simple. Most of the time, it works. I bet the same is true here. The clue sounds really confusing, but what if the answer is something simple?"

Stanley looked at Felix. "You getting any reception on your phone to search for some simple answers?"

Felix took out his phone and studied it. He held the power button down, then shook his head. "Nah. It wasn't just Evan's phone that got knocked out. Mine won't even turn on. None of ours will, I bet. I wonder if MacBeth hit us with an electromagnetic pulse or something."

"Then why does this one still work?" asked Stanley, holding up the phone they found in the crater.

"If I had to guess," said Felix, "MacBeth turned that one off remotely before hitting the EM pulse, then turned it back on afterwards."

"Boy, this guy is determined," said Gertie. "And crazy. Anybody want to take bets on who it is, anyway? Because I have an idea—"

"I think we all do," said Stanley. "But frankly, I'm trying to put that out of my mind right now. If we don't think clearly, we're going to miss something important. And if we don't have internet access, we're going to have to do this the old fashioned way. Charlotte's on to something about keeping it simple. Rack your brains. Think of anything with a common pairing of 1 and 8, 18 x 7, or 126. Just say whatever comes into your heads. There are no dumb answers here."

"When I was 7, I lost my first tooth," said Felix.

"Are you sure there's no such thing as dumb answers?" said Gertie.

"Voting age is 18," offered Charlotte.

"Okay," said Gertie, "but how does that help us?"

"Chemistry," said Herman.

"I'm planning on having 7 kids and living until I'm 126," said Felix.

"Chemistry," Herman repeated.

"I'll probably keep dying my hair red," said Felix. "I'll never look a day over 81."

"Now I *know* there are such things as dumb answers," said Gertie.

Stanley held up a hand. "Herman, what do you mean chemistry?"

Herman flushed. "Well, before I started hanging out with you guys, I was trying to get into the Science Club. I didn't know anything about science, really, so I did a little research for their interview."

"There are interviews to join the Science Club?" asked Gertie.

"Yeah," said Herman. "They're pretty serious about...well, everything. Anyway, the day of the interview was when you guys called me about tracking down the Grinch. I never rescheduled with them. It wouldn't have worked anyway. I don't have a good mind for book stuff."

"Plus, you like to spray paint dogs blue," said Felix.

"And there's that," agreed Herman. "The Science Club kids are more of the rule following type. Anyway, I do remember one thing from all that studying. The period table has 7 rows and 18 columns of thingees on it."

"You mean elements?" asked Stanley.

Herman shrugged. "Sure."

"How many elements are there?" asked Gertie.

Herman shrugged again. "I'd only gotten as far as memorizing the number of rows and columns."

"We need to verify this," said Stanley. He looked at the phone in his hand. "Maybe this is internet capable." He pressed a few buttons then shook his head. "Felix, you know more about chemistry than the rest of us. Is he right?"

Felix shrugged. "Unfortunately, I don't have a photographic memory. Luckily, a friend of mine does. Charlotte, blink your eyes a couple times and call up the periodic table of elements."

"Eidetic memory," said Charlotte.

"And that's different than photographic memory how?" said Herman.

"Photographic memory is just great recall for

specific details. Eidetic memory is the ability to recall pictures of things I've seen and heard. Then all I have to do it study the picture for whatever I'm looking for."

"So call up the picture and get studying," said Felix.

Charlotte tapped the side of her head. "No picture of periodic tables in here. Sorry."

"Maybe we don't need it," said Stanley. "Herman, do your best to draw it from memory."

Herman raised an eyebrow when Gertie handed him the notebook, but he began to draw. He gave the completed sketch to Stanley and mumbled, "Best I can do."

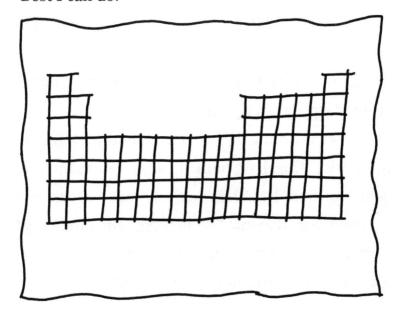

"I'll take your best any day," said Stanley. "Besides, right now we don't have much of a choice. Felix, what do you think?"

Felix examined the sketch. "It looks right to me. That means 7 down, 18 across, and 118 elements."

Gertie nodded. "It's a table of 18 x 7 that doesn't equal 126. That would fit the clue, but what does it reveal about a common pairing of 1 and 8?"

"Now let me think," said Felix. "Each element of the periodic table is presented in order of increasing atomic number, its number of protons. Number 1 is H, or Hydrogen."

"What's number 8?" Stanley said hopefully.

"Oxygen," said Felix. "So, class, what's a common pairing of Hydrogen and Oxygen?"

"H20," blurted Gertie. "That's water. Finally, score one chemistry point for me."

"Water is about the most common molecule in the world," Charlotte smiled. "Like I said, the trail would be simple." Then her eyes got big and she snapped her fingers. "Remember our circle that started at the point (-2,3) and had a radius of 2? Now I know what is exactly 2 miles away from

Farmer Dahlgren's crater."

Charlotte said no more. She just charged forward into the woods and Stanley called after her. "But what does it all mean?"

"It means the next clue is at Lake Beverly. We got another mile to go so we better get moving."

CHAPTER EIGHT

THE TESTS WITHIN

The terrain wasn't easy for Stanley, Felix, and especially Gertie, and soon Herman and Charlotte were outpacing them. But eventually, the friends came out of the woods and reached a beautiful mountain lake. Lake Beverly was fed by crystal clear snowmelt running down from the Adirondack Mountains that banked it on one side.

There was nobody else on the lake. No hikers. No fishermen. Just five kids trying to follow the clue of a madman.

"Here," said Charlotte, opening her bag. "Let's refill the canteens. The water from the mountains is pristine." The others rested while she and Herman walked down the bank in search of a stream.

Stanley sat on a rock and shook pebbles out of his shoes. Just as he finished lacing them, he heard Charlotte scream his name. Gertie and Felix sprinted after him towards the voice. When they reached Charlotte and Herman, they saw a small rowboat tied up to the bank.

Herman stood in the middle of it. He reached down and grabbed a bright yellow paper duct taped to the bottom of the boat. He read it aloud.

Clue # 4
Row and Climb, one and all.
Search then Find, until you....

"Until we what?" said Gertie.

"It probably rhymes with *all*," said Charlotte.

"Mall," suggested Felix.

Gertie rolled her eyes. "Well done. You've solved it, Felix. We search for the clue until we *mall*."

"How about *call*?" said Stanley. "Maybe the phone will start working once we climb whatever it is we're supposed to climb."

"If we have to row," Herman said, "it looks like we're headed out there." He pointed to an island in the middle of Lake Beverly. It was a rocky mass of pine trees and boulders and looked to be about the size of a football field. At its center was a tall hill.

"There aren't any others islands around that I know of," said Charlotte. "I bet you're right."

"Riddles and water," said Felix as they clambered into the small rowboat. "Anyone else feel like they're in *The Hobbit* right now?"

Gertie laid the oars at his feet. "You're rowing, Gollum. At least we get to sit down for a change."

It was slow going, and Charlotte and Felix switched off rowing several times before they reached the island. Herman jumped into knee-deep water and tied the boat to a fallen tree on the rocky beach. Then they all unloaded and started climbing up boulders, navigating around trees, leaping over streams, and making their way to the top of the hill at the center of the island. About ten minutes later they stood together at the top looking down at the mainland.

"Well," said Stanley, checking the phone, "this thing still isn't making any calls. We'd better get looking for the next clue. It's gotta be at the top of this hill somewhere."

Gertie sat down on a large boulder and sighed. "We're at the wrong place. Maybe we were supposed to *row* to the other side of the lake and *climb* the Adirondacks where we could *search* and *find* until we *ball*, or *doll*, or *stall* or—oh no, I just figured it out. Everybody get off the hill now!"

But it was too late. There was a loud snap, then

complete confusion.

Stanley had just enough time to grab onto a newly formed ridge as the ground under his feet collapsed. All at once Gertie and Herman disappeared down a gaping hole. Felix screamed and plunged in after them. Charlotte clung to a root, but she was slipping into the blackness.

"Charlotte," screamed Stanley. "Hold on. I'll pull myself up and come get you."

Charlotte looked down between her dangling feet and back up at him. "No, Stanley. Just let go." Then she disappeared.

Stanley tried to pull himself up, but his foot slipped and he tumbled after his friends. He fell for about eight feet, hit solid ground, and slid down a long stone tunnel. He screamed his head off until finally he landed on something surprisingly soft.

"Oww!" said Felix.

Stanley stumbled to his feet as his friends untangled themselves from each other.

"*Fall*," said Gertie. "Search then find, until you *fall*. Just for the record, I'm not a big fan of MacBeth."

"Sure it was MacBeth?" asked Herman. "Maybe that was some kind of animal trap."

"That was no animal trap." Charlotte's voice carried from farther down the tunnel. "It was definitely MacBeth."

"What makes you so sure?" asked Herman.

"Because he left us this." Charlotte waved a long black flashlight and clicked it on. "It had a little yellow love note attached to it."

With my compliments. Your friend,
MacBeth.

"I really hate this guy," said Stanley.

"Well," said Charlotte, looking up at the hole in the ceiling, "I'd pull the plug on all this right now, but there's no chance we're getting back up that way."

"Agreed," said Stanley. "Better follow the tunnel and find another way out. Herman, you go last and make sure everybody stays together. Charlotte, lead the way."

They wove through narrow tunnels for half an hour before coming upon a large cavern with a small pond at its center bordered by gray sand. Light streamed in from an unseen opening high overhead and illuminated long stalactites hanging down like knobby fingers.

"Now I'm starting to feel like a Hobbit," said Gertie. "You guys remember that scene where Frodo meets Gollum in the cave?"

"Yeah," said Felix. "I never thought I'd say this, but I'm actually sick of the Hobbit motif. Unless someone's got second breakfast. Second breakfast would change everything."

"Hey," said Gertie, "what's that?"

They followed Gertie's point to their left where a small black tape recorder sat on top of a large rock. A little yellow sticky note on the recorder read:

Play Me.

Gertie pressed play. MacBeth's voice crackled through the small speakers and echoed off the cavernous walls.

"Congratulations, Math Inspectors. I do hope you know how much entertainment you have given me. Although you have to admit, as much fun as they were, this morning's exercises were pretty simple.

Simple they were, but highly instructive too. So I thank you for playing along.

"And now we move to the more challenging portion of today's game. The clues are over, and the tests have begun. I prepared a little something special for each of you.

"But before I reveal the first test, remember what I told you this morning. I do not often repeat myself, so listen carefully: Each test will ask more than you may be willing to give, but you can walk away at any time. Simply follow the tunnel to its end, and an exit will present itself. You can be home in time for the big show this afternoon.

"And remember, if you choose to quit, you walk away with respect. Not my respect, of course, but no one in this pitiful little town is going to think any differently of you. And now the time to decide has arrived. Happy choosing, Math Inspectors. And may the true genius among us carry the day.

"If you are ready for the first test,
it is time to ask:
Can you reach and grab? What a simple task.
But there is only one who can pay this fee:
So how badly does he want that key?"

CHAPTER NINE

THE KEY

The voice stopped, and Gertie turned off the tape recorder. "Okay, well that was super creepy."

"You know what always uncreeps me?" said Felix. "Second breakfast. Charlotte, you wouldn't happen to have a sausage and egg burrito in the magical bag of food would you?"

Charlotte glared at him.

"Right. Me shut up or me get hurt."

"What was that grating noise?" Herman asked.

"I didn't hear anything," said Stanley.

Herman pointed to a ledge behind them and about 8 feet off the ground. "I heard something metal open up there just as the voice stopped."

Charlotte flashed the light up at the ledge. It was a small opening, about two feet wide and six inches tall, like a stone shelf cut into the wall.

"It looks like a skinny pizza oven," said Felix. "Maybe MacBeth has some sort of evil delivery business."

Charlotte tossed Herman the flashlight and jumped up on the wall. She caught the ledge with one hand and pulled herself up just enough to look over it. "It's hard to see anything in there clearly. I think there's a cage in the wall. It sounds like things are scampering around in there. Like rats or possibly—"

"Squirrels!" screamed Felix jumping into the air. When he landed he started shaking. "Th-th-those are squirrels. C-c-can't you tell? Those are squirrel feet. I hear them in my nightmares all the time."

Herman threw up his hands. "I really don't understand the squirrel thing."

"And you wouldn't," screamed Felix. "Because you're not one of the chosen few people whom squirrels have sworn to hunt down and destroy. But I am. They stalk me at night. They steal my chips while I'm on stakeouts. They harass me in my own tree house. And why? I don't know. Maybe it's my stunning good looks, my wonderful smell, or my wicked charm. Heck, we may never know. But what I do know is squirrels are evil, and I'll bet dollars to donuts—and I really love donuts—that just behind that rock ledge is a flock of squirrels."

"I don't think they're called a flock," said Gertie.

"Death squad? Is death squad better?" squealed Felix.

"Um, I was thinking small adorable family, or something like that," said Gertie.

Felix shook his head. "Gertie, Gertie, Gertie. Cute, little, adorable Gertie. Someday when the only things left on earth are squirrels and machines, then, maybe then, you'll—" Felix froze. His eyes opened wide and his face turned ghostly white. He began shaking again.

"Felix?" Gertie said. "Felix, what's wrong with you?"

Felix swallowed so hard Stanley could see a lump travel all the way down his giraffe sized throat. Then he pointed his enormous index finger at the rocky squirrel cage. "MacBeth said he had a test for each of us. I think this test is for me. J-j-just me."

Felix sat down on a rock, grabbed a fist-full of red curls in each hand and shook his head. "None of you can help here," he said. "I know what I need to do. It's either man up and face the squirrel death squad, or the Hamilton Roller Coaster goes BOOM!"

Stanley looked at the ledge and heard the little squeaks coming from behind its stone face. "Maybe not. Charlotte, give me a boost up there and let me take a look."

"It's no use, I tell you," sobbed Felix.

"Just let me check it out," said Stanley. "Flashlight, please."

Charlotte made a sturdy back and Stanley, with Gertie and Herman steadying him, just managed to peek over the ledge.

"Okay," he said. "So, yes, you were right. There looks to be about a hundred squirrels in a cage behind the stone ledge."

"Are they vicious looking?" asked Felix.

"Actually," said Stanley, "it looks like MacBeth went out of his way to get the world's smallest, cutest, and frankly most adorable squirrels I've ever seen. I think this one just offered me a nut."

"Probably a ploy to share his cute little rabies with you," said Felix.

"I don't think squirrels get rabies," said Herman.

"Look, I appreciate you all lying to me to make me feel better," said Felix. "But I know what I have to do. And since it's the last time you'll be seeing me alive, I really could use that sausage and egg burrito."

"I can't quite tell what it is," said Stanley, standing on his tiptoes for a better view. "But there's a blue light coming from the back of the cage. And there's something else just hanging there right by it. If I can reach through the squirrels, I might be able to grab it."

Stanley tried every which way to wedge his arm into the hole, but, even with the added length of the flashlight, his arm wasn't long enough to reach the object before his shoulder hit the opening of the ledge. Finally he gave up, jumped to the ground, and shook his head.

Felix mumbled to himself. "They're just furry little minions that want to bring about the destruction of the world. What's so terrible about that? I can do this. I can do this. I can do this."

Gertie looked at Stanley. "Felix can't do this. You

know how squirrels are with him. They'll eat him alive. And even if they don't, he'll never be the same. Can't one of us get whatever that is?"

Stanley shrugged. "Not by grabbing it. None of you have arms any longer than mine."

"Why don't we just scoop the squirrels out of there?" suggested Herman. "I've got experience with small critters. Or maybe find a stick."

Stanley shook his head. "It'd take time we don't have to get all of them out of there. And unless we find something about a foot longer than this flashlight lying around here, nobody but Felix can get anywhere near it."

"It's the key," said Felix. "Don't you remember what the message on the tape recorder said: '*So how badly does he want that key?*' I'm the *he,* and that thing in there is the *key.* Where's Buckets when I need him? Oh Buckets," Felix shouted. "I forgive you for taking my food, old buddy. I get it, birthday cake is delicious. If I were you, I would have stolen it too."

"There's gotta be another way," said Gertie.

Felix jumped up and let out a very weird sound.

"You don't get it, do you? This MacSquirrel guy is coming up with tests for each one of us. I'm the only one who is terrified of squirrels. And I'm the only one with long enough arms to pull this off. It's either me or nobody."

Stanley put a hand on Felix's shoulder. "You don't have to do this. We can follow the tunnel, and get off this island, and let the cops figure this out."

Felix took a few steps down the tunnel and stared into its empty blackness. But a minute later he came back. He took the flashlight. "I do have to do this. MacBeth made things personal this morning when he took out Creepy. What did we get into this business for anyway, if not to stop bad guys? We all have to make sacrifices, Stanley. Good luck to you all when your time comes." He looked at Charlotte and nodded. She braced herself against the wall and cupped her hands like a stirrup. Felix put one foot in and looked back at them. "Last chance for anybody with a sausage burrito in their pocket to produce it. Nobody? Okay, well this is how it all ends."

Charlotte gave him a three count and boosted him up the wall. Felix's body was shaking worse than a cottonwood in a thunderstorm, but he was standing straight and peering over the stone ledge.

"How's it going up there?" asked Stanley.

Felix seemed frozen.

"Felix?"

"Let's try something else," said Gertie.

"No," Felix said. He snapped off the flashlight and dropped it to Herman. "I just can't handle seeing all of their little beady eyes staring at me. I've come this far, and these rabid little rodents aren't going to stop me now. Besides, I just remembered something. It's Felix time!"

Felix reared back his head and let out a piercing yell that echoed off the stone walls, "For the roller coaster of my youth!" Then he stared into the hole and let out a long breath before plunging his arm, all the way up to his armpit, into the cage of squirrels.

CHAPTER TEN

EXPLOSIVE!

Felix pulled his arm out of the cage. He stared into the dark hole, unmoving. But a key with a blue light attached to it dangled from his hand.

"Great job, Felix," said Charlotte. "But believe it or not, you're getting a little heavy. Want to hurry it up and step down?"

Felix continued to stare into the dark hole in the wall.

"Better get him down," said Stanley. "Here, Herman, take his other hand. That's right. Now, you just sit right here, Felix. You did good. Really, really good. Now let go of the key. Let-go-Felix. That's right. Gertie, see what you can do."

Gertie had a hand on each of Felix's shoulders and was staring straight into his eyes. She started talking to him, shaking his shoulders, snapping her fingers right in front of his face. Nothing.

"So that's it?" Charlotte pointed. "That's the key to diffuse the bombs on the roller coaster?"

"I guess so," said Stanley. "It's not exactly what I was expecting. It's kind of old fashioned and clunky."

There's something wrapped around it," said Herman.

Stanley turned over the key. Another piece of yellow paper. He unrolled it.

> *Felix has made his choice;*
> *Round the pond to face another.*
> *Sometimes the last to join is first to leave;*
> *You cannot Hyde forever.*

Herman snatched the paper from Stanley. "*You cannot Hyde forever,*" Herman said. Then he closed his eyes, shook his head, and struck out around the pond.

The pond in the center of the cavern proved to be sizeable. It took close to ten minutes to reach the other side since the group was slowed down by Felix, who had not yet recovered from his strange case of squirrel shock and was unresponsive to their questions.

"I see something up there," said Charlotte. "Come on, Herman."

The two of them ran ahead and huddled over

something on the ground, while Gertie and Stanley brought Felix along between them.

"We'd better figure out a way to open it from a distance," Stanley heard Charlotte said.

"I don't think so," said Herman.

Charlotte pointed. "It's marked *EXPLOSIVE!*"

Herman nodded. "And if it's what I think it is, it *is* explosive. Just not the way you're imagining."

Stanley sat Felix on a large rock about ten yards away and joined them. "Did you say explosive?"

Charlotte shrugged. "See for yourself."

The thing on the ground was a big leather trunk, bolted shut with a padlock. And the word *EXPLOSIVE!* was painted in large blue letters on the outside.

Gertie joined them. "From the note on the key, there's some sort of choice we have to make about it," she said.

"Yeah," said Herman. "At least, *I* have a choice to make." Herman stuck his hand out to Stanley. "Mind giving me the key and a little space?"

Stanley pulled the key out of his pocket and nodded at the others. "Come on, guys. Let's see what Felix is up to."

"Felix isn't going anywhere," said Gertie, "and I want to know what's in the trunk."

"No," said Charlotte. "Stanley's right. Let's give Herman some space."

Stanley, Charlotte, and Gertie walked back to Felix and sat down.

Herman fell to his knees in front of the trunk. He inserted the key into the padlock and turned it until something clicked. Then he took the top of the trunk with both hands and stopped. He let out a long breath and slowly swung the trunk open. Instantly, papers fell to the ground all around him.

"What gives?" Gertie whispered.

Stanley shook his head. "It'll be his to tell or nobody's."

After a few minutes, Gertie whispered, "How long do we wait?"

"Not long," said a quiet voice. It was Herman's. "You guys can come back. I've made my choice."

Stanley and the girls walked over to the trunk.

Gertie picked up the first piece of paper she came to. "This is a newspaper article. About the town water tower and how somebody painted a blue smiley face on it. And—wait a second. Here's another one about the half-shaved dog. And the mice in tutus, and the car mechanic, and—what's all that in the trunk?"

Herman held up a handful of items without looking any of his friends in the face. "Photos, clippings, crime scene investigation paperwork. It's pretty much a treasure chest of evidence on my old friend, Mr. Jekyll. And this was on top." He held up a yellow piece of paper.

Stanley took it from him and read:

How heavy the secret so many years carried;
But here is your chance to start anew.
End the game now and your past shall be buried;
No more running from crimes in blue.
Or dial the year your parents were married;
And confess your crimes to receive the next clue.

"MacBeth knows who I am," said Herman.

"You mean he knows about your little misdeeds?" said Gertie.

"I think it's worse than that," said Herman. "I mean MacBeth knows me. He knows this is not just about me getting into a little trouble with the law."

"Then what does it mean?" asked Charlotte.

"I haven't told you guys this, but the reason my folks moved to Ravensburg last year was because of all the trouble I'd gotten into when we lived in the city. So when I got kicked out of Sunshine Magnet before the first two months of school had even gone by...well they told me one more mix up this year and I'd be sent off to a military school."

"Wait," said Gertie. "You mean there really is such a thing as military school? I thought that was only in movies."

"They're real," said Herman. "To tell you the truth, before I met you guys I didn't really care where they sent me. But now—but all that's beside the point. I've already made up my mind. Give me the phone, Stanley."

"Whoa, whoa, whoa," said Stanley. "This is not what you signed up for, Herman. Let's think this through a minute."

"Yeah," said Gertie, pumping her fists. "If MacBeth thinks he can come in here and split us up so easily, he's got another thing coming. We will not be intimidated."

"You can talk all you want, guys. And, well, thanks for wanting to. But this is my choice."

"It's not a fair choice," said Charlotte.

"But it's mine," said Herman. "And it's not just about the roller coaster. That line about the weight of a secret is true. Do you know what it's like to wake up every morning and wonder if this is the day your past is going to catch up with you? If there's one thing I know for sure, it's that things like what's in this trunk can never be buried forever. Stanley, give me the phone."

Stanley hesitated. But he handed it over, and Herman entered the digits for the year his parents were married, 2-0-0-1. The code seemed to activate a dialing program and a ten-digit phone number appeared on the screen.

Stanley looked at it. "It's a Ravensburg number, but I don't recognize it." Nobody else did either.

Herman hit the send button and punched down the speaker key. After two dial tones, someone answered.

"This is Ravensburg Police Chief Abrams speaking. Who is this?"

"Chief Abrams, this is Herman Dale, and I am Mr. Jekyll."

There was a long pause. Finally Chief Abrams sighed. "I received an unmarked letter minutes ago saying somebody was going to call my private phone and confess to a crime. I have to say, I was hoping it would be a bigger fish than a middle-school vandal."

Herman said, "MacBeth's last clue promised if I confessed, we would receive another clue. Do you have it?"

"Not that you aren't going to feel the long arm of

the law all over your legal backside, young man," the chief blustered. "You caused my officers and me quite a bit of trouble a few months back, and believe me when I say that disobeying me again today and running off is not going to earn you any fans around here."

"Chief Abrams," said Stanley. "I'll take full responsibility for running off today. But we have a lead on the key to diffuse the bombs, and we are running out of time."

"I thought I told you I only wanted you kids to run interference," said the chief.

"So you've figured out how to diffuse the bomb?"

"That's not the point—"

"Right now, it is the point, Chief. The best thing we can do is to play this game out. Now, do you have a clue for us or not?"

The chief seemed to consider something for a minute. Then he sighed again. "Fine, on the back of this letter it says something strange."

Billy Bones will show you the way.

"Billy Bones?" said Gertie. "I know that name. That's a rock band, right?"

"A rock band," blurted the chief. "You kids need to get out of your math books and into some good stories now and then. Like those English Club kids. They'd know who Billy Bones is."

"So who is he?" said Gertie.

The chief could barely control his temper. "Only one of the greatest characters from the greatest book ever— *Treasure Island*."

"Oh, right," said Stanley, "I've seen the Muppets movie. I think I can take it from here."

"Muppets! Of all the math-loving foolishness—"

"Chief, send a couple cars to meet us as Farmer Dahlgren's place. We'll be there as soon as we can." Stanley hit the end call button. "And actually, I agree with him, guys. We could stand to beef up our knowledge of the Classics. But we've got the whole summer. In the meantime, I need something sharp."

Charlotte produced a Swiss Army Knife.

"That should do it," said Stanley. "Slice the inside of the trunk's lid. That's what Billy Bones does in *Treasure Island* to find the hidden treasure map."

The trunk was lined with leather on the inside,

too, but after a minute Charlotte was able to puncture the lining enough to get a finger inside and tear a large hole in it. After fishing around the corners, she pulled out the now familiar yellow paper and unfolded it. She looked at it and turned white.

CHAPTER ELEVEN

THE DIVE

Stanley put a hand on Charlotte's shoulder and took the yellow piece of paper from her. He turned to the others and read it.

What you have been searching for all day
Is now just a single swim away.
The real key is in a box of silver and black,
Two minutes there and two minutes back.
But, if you are as clever at math as you claim,
You will solve the riddle and win the game.
Look around. This is no time for frowning.
After all, what is worth the risk of drowning?

Stanley and Gertie looked at each other, then at Charlotte. She was still white.

"I think I can do it." Charlotte said.

"You can hold your breath for four minutes?" said Herman. "And how do we know this is even meant for you?"

Charlotte didn't answer.

"Two reasons," said Stanley in a voice just above a whisper. "Charlotte is the best swimmer in Ravensburg Middle School. And, it's what she fears the most."

"Swimming?" asked Herman.

"No," Charlotte nodded her head. "Not swimming. Drowning."

"I'm not sure I follow," said Herman.

Charlotte crouched down next to the pond and swept her hand across the surface. "My mom drowned when I was little. Dad put me in swimming lessons right after that, and I've never been afraid of swimming. But that didn't help shake the fear of...um, you know."

"Well, this is one fear you are not going to have to face," said Stanley. "It's my turn to say this, I'm pulling the plug on the whole thing. Hamilton Roller Coaster or not, I know the answer to the riddle. Nothing. Nothing is worth *you* drowning."

Charlotte stood up, crossed her arms, and set her feet apart. "Stanley, I'm not going to be the only person who doesn't face her fears today. You might be my best friend, but I'm going in there and there's nothing you can do to stop me."

Stanley jumped up, sprinted between Charlotte and the water, and stared straight into her eyes. "I might not look like much, but you'll be surprised what happens if you come a step closer to that water."

"Wait a minute, you two," said Gertie. "I've been rereading the clue. I think we're missing something here."

"Right now all we're doing is wasting time," said Charlotte.

"No, this is important," Gertie pointed at the riddle. "Stanley already solved this part— *what is worth the risk of drowning?* The answer is nothing."

"Move, Stanley," said Charlotte. "The sooner I get this over with, the sooner we move on."

Herman had moved shoulder to shoulder with Stanley, and Charlotte looked like she was measuring her next move.

"You guys, listen to me," screamed Gertie. "It's a riddle. *Nothing* is worth drowning for. That's the answer. And the other line says: *But if you are as clever at math as you claim, You will discover the trick and win the game.* So what's the trick?"

"I'm going to count to three, Stanley. You and Herman have until then to step aside," said Charlotte.

"Why aren't any of you listening to me?" squealed Gertie. She ran over to Felix and snapped in his face. "Felix, wake up. I need your help." She snapped again. Nothing. No reaction.

"One..." Charlotte said.

Gertie slapped Felix's face. Blankness.

"Two..."

With all her might, Gertie shook Felix by the shoulders and screamed into his face, "Where are you when I need you, you Big Red Beanpole?"

"Three!" said Charlotte.

At that moment, Felix jumped to his feet and yelled, "I'd like one extra-large Belcher Special, please, smothered in chocolate raspberry sauce."

The others were so astounded at his recovery that they stared at him in amazement.

"Felix, you're back," said Gertie, wrapping both arms

around him. Then she punched him in the shoulder. "Where have you been? I need your help here."

"Whoa," said Felix, "it's all coming back to me. I was up there on that wall staring down the mouths of those furry little meat grinders when I realized there was only one chance in the world I was going to be able to stick my arm in there. I had to make my mind go completely blank. So, I gathered my thoughts, pretended I was in front of Under Doggies hot dog stand, and prepared to order. You know how I can turn off my brain when I'm in line for Under Doggies, right? Well, it worked. I've been waiting in line for a long time, though. Which one of you called me out?"

"That must have been me," said Gertie. "Mr. Under likes to call you Big Red Beanpole, too. You must have thought it was time to order."

"Thanks, Gertie. But now I'm starving. Do we have anything to eat? And what's been happening since I checked out?"

"Basically, Herman turned himself in to Chief Abrams for the Jekyll crimes, and Charlotte here is trying to drown herself."

"Wow," said Felix, running a hand through his moppy red hair. "So, a lot."

"But we are not going to let her," said Stanley.

"They don't have a choice," said Charlotte. "As I was just about to make clear to them when you woke up. And I'm not going to drown."

"Look, Charlotte," said Gertie. "I have one request. Listen to me while I reread this clue. If you're not satisfied with what I have to say about it, I'll help you into the water myself. Deal?"

"Fine," said Charlotte. "But hurry up. We don't have all day."

"Listen," began Gertie, "the note doesn't actually say that you have to swim at all. But it does say *look around,* and *solve the riddle.* I'm telling you, there's something here we're missing. We can math our way out of this somehow."

"Did I mention I really hate this guy?" said Stanley.

"About fifty times," said Charlotte. "But I'm not convinced I don't need to swim."

Stanley looked at his watch. "It's worth looking into. Charlotte, once we get the key, how long do you think it will take us to get from here back to Old Man Dahlgren's place?

"About 10 minutes to the shore if we're rowing at top speed. Then another 15 minutes back to his farm. But who knows how long it'll take us to get out of this place."

Stanley nodded. "Right. Even then, assuming we can get a car, how long from Dahlgren's to Hamilton Amusement Park?"

"Another fifteen minutes."

"I'd rather not cut it so close. So let's say we have to find that key and get out of this cave by 2:15 at the latest. That means we've got a little under an hour to figure this problem out."

"Fine," said Charlotte, stepping back from the pond. "I'll give you half an hour. But that's it."

"It's a good thing you're not stubborn," said Stanley. He looked around. "I've asked this a lot today, but does anybody have any ideas?"

"Maybe there's some way to use math to reduce the water between the shore and the tunnel," said Felix.

Huh?" said Herman.

"Water displacement. That's based on mathematics, right?" Felix pointed to a stack of boulders against one wall of the cave. "What if we find a way to get those boulders moving, they land in the water, displace the water, and bam, Charlotte doesn't have as much water to swim through."

Stanley shook his head. "We'd risk covering up the tunnel. But it's a good idea. Gertie, hand everybody a piece of paper from your notebook. Herman, can you spare some writing utensils? I wish we were back in the tree house, but this will have to do. Everybody search the area and see what you can come up with."

The kids worked on every idea they could consider. But, as time dragged on, they kept getting more and more frustrated. Stanley looked at his watch. They were running out of time.

Charlotte stood up. "Looks like we don't have any other choice."

"Charlotte," said Stanley, "MacBeth has designed the swim to fail. It can't be done. That's the whole point."

"Stanley, our town has the oldest roller coaster in the country. The *entire* country. But it's more than that. I'm not going to let this guy get the better of me. I been working some calculations of my own, and I think I can do this."

"Charlotte!" said Stanley.

"Hear me out. I know I can hold my breath long enough to dive and find the box. I've been free diving in mountain lakes with my dad plenty of times, and I know I can do that. But you're right, I might not have enough breath to get back. Stanley, you're the next best swimmer after me. At three minutes, you dive down and look for me. Gertie and Felix, one minute after Stanley dives down, you guys follow. Get me of the water, and start doing chest compressions like they do in CPR."

"That's nuts," said Stanley.

Gertie shook her head. "I'm telling you Charlotte, that's not the right solution to the problem."

"But right now, it's the only solution we have."

Stanley balled up his fists and stomped away. This was his fault. There was something about this problem that he just wasn't seeing, and now his friend was going to put her life in jeopardy because of it. He looked back. Charlotte was sitting down, eyes closed, slowing her breathing, getting ready to dive.

Stanley kicked a rock in front of him and watched it skitter across the cave floor. He chased after it about to kick it again when he stopped and stared down at the ground.

The rock had landed next to some other rocks. And these rocks weren't a random collection of rocks. They'd been positioned. But not in letters, or numbers, or words. In piles. Stanley was sure of it.

On the right, there was one rock. Then a foot over, another rock. Then a foot over, two rocks. Then a foot over, three rocks. Then a foot over, five rocks.

Then a foot over, eight rocks. And then one more foot over, thirteen rocks. And that's where the pattern stopped. But it was enough. Stanley recognized this pattern. He counted again, just to make sure his brain wasn't playing tricks on him.

"Stanley," Charlotte said. "I'm going in. Be sure to come after me in three minutes."

Stanley whipped around and found Charlotte on the edge of the pond. Even from here, he could see her chest heave back and forth as she took in several large breaths.

"Stop Charlotte, STOP!" Stanley yelled, waving his arms as he ran towards her. "I have something to show you."

CHAPTER TWELVE

THE GOLDEN KEY

Charlotte paused at the water's edge.

Gertie, Felix, and Herman ran to join Stanley. He pointed at the rocks and looked at his friends for confirmation.

"That's the Fibonacci sequence all right," said Gertie.

Charlotte walked over and nodded her head. "Agreed. But what does Fibonacci have to do with solving our problem?"

"And what the heck is a Fiber...whatever sequence?" asked Herman. "All I see are piles of rocks."

"The Fibonacci sequence," said Stanley. "It's a famous series of numbers where the next number in the sequence is the sum of the previous two numbers. And I don't know what it means yet, but it's definitely a clue. Everybody, spread around the cavern. Look for anything that doesn't look random. Anything that looks like it was done on purpose. MacBeth is trying to tell us something, and Gertie was right, we *can* math our way out of this one."

The five friends searched around the cavern. Two minutes later, Gertie's voice echoed off the walls, "Got something."

They rushed over to where she was pointing. On the wall was a rectangle, drawn in red chalk. But this rectangle was odd. It had a single green line through it, dividing it into a square on one side and a smaller rectangle on the other.

"So what does that mean?" asked Herman.

"I have no idea," said Stanley. "I can't think of any connection with this shape and Fibonacci. But maybe there's something else around here that ties it together."

Charlotte looked down at her watch. "We're running out of time, Stanley."

"I know. Just trust me. Keep looking."

A minute later it was Herman who yelled. When they got to him, he was on all fours tracing something with his forefinger. "Right here, someone has drawn a star in the sand."

"It's not just any star," said Gertie. "The mathematical term is pentagram. We've got the Fibonacci sequence, a rectangle with a line through it, and now a pentagram. How do any of those help us get the key from the bottom of the pond?"

Stanley pushed his glasses up the bridge of his nose. He was thinking. Really thinking. And when he did that, he needed quiet. He was puzzling it over in his mind. Then, another thought occurred to him.

"MacBeth is clever," Stanley said. "And he doesn't say things by mistake. The clue says that the key is at the bottom of the pond in a silver and black box. But notice what it *doesn't* say. It doesn't say that the *only* key is in that box. As Gertie reminded us, there is a trick to getting the key. What if there is a key in the box, but there's also another way of getting it. What if everything we need is right here in these mathematical clues?"

Charlotte looked at him. "How sure are you, Stanley? I've got to dive now for us to have any chance of getting that bomb diffused before 3 pm."

"Let me show you. Then you can judge for yourself." Stanley ran over to the rectangle. "I wondered where I had seen this rectangle before. But we've all seen it in our math books." He picked up a jagged rock and drew the letter a and letter b at different parts of the rectangle.

"Does anybody recognize it now?" he asked.

"Oh," Gertie said, "that section on ratios we did last month. It's when you divide a number by another number."

"Yes," Stanley circled the entire shape, "but usually this rectangle is used to talk about a very famous ratio. The Golden Ratio, known as Phi, or the number known as approximately 1.618. A ratio famous because it appears all over in nature and in mathematics. For instance—"

"The pentagram," Felix said. "The edges of a true pentagram are in Golden Ratio with each other. If you took the length of an edge of a pentagram and then divided it by the edge with the next greatest length, the ratio between the two would be 1.618."

"Exactly," agreed Stanley, "but that's not all. The Fibonacci sequence has ratios as well. The ratios of a term with the term right before it. And, anybody want to guess what ratio you get closer and closer to the further you go out in the Fibonacci sequence?"

"Wait," Herman said, "let me do this one. Is it 1.618?"

"Yep, the Golden Ratio. Guys, this whole time we've thought the key to diffusing the bomb was an actual key. What if it's not? What if all we would find in that box is a yellow piece of paper with the Golden Ratio on it? Guys, the key is a number. It's the Golden Ratio. It's 1.618."

"That's an incredible risk to take," said Charlotte.

"Yes," said Stanley. "But that *is* a risk I'm willing to take."

Charlotte smiled. "Thanks, Stanley. And, come to think of it, when I recall the images of the bombs, I see something on them that could be a keypad."

"Then let's get out of here and save that roller coaster," said Gertie.

The Math Inspectors followed the path into the mouth of a small tunnel. At first, the tunnel was wide enough for two people to walk side-by-side. Soon, however, the walls narrowed, and as they walked on there were times Felix had to twist and fold his lanky arms and legs just to squeeze through tight spots.

Stanley followed Felix, who followed Gertie, who followed Charlotte, while Herman took his place at the rear. Suddenly Charlotte shot the flashlight from right to left and yelled, "Everybody stop!" But it was a moment too late, and Stanley found himself in the middle of another pileup after sliding down a small incline and landing in a heap at the edge of something solid.

"Yep," said Charlotte, "that's what I thought. The end of the line."

Felix untwisted somebody's leg from his neck. "Didn't MacPsycho say there'd be a door at the end of the tunnel?"

"No," said Charlotte. "He said an exit would *present itself* at the end of the tunnel."

"Maybe this will help," said Herman. "It wedged in my ear when I collided with the wall."

Charlotte shined the light on Herman, who was holding a piece of yellow paper. He unrolled it and read it aloud.

Come to this place still on a quest?
Or did a weak link break from its test?
To home and safety you are free to go,
Or back to the park to finish the show.
The exit I promised is your next goal,
But we have yet to discuss its toll.
The door allows all but one to go through,
Since, for an operator, only a Dead Man will do.

CHAPTER THIRTEEN

DEAD MAN'S SWITCH

"Well this strange day just turned spooky," said Herman. "Only a Dead Man can work the door? I don't get it."

Gertie snatched the clue out of Herman's hand. "You gotta be kidding me," she said. "This is *my* test."

"How do you know that?" asked Charlotte.

Gertie crossed her short arms. "The Dead Man is, pardon the pun, the dead giveaway."

"But what's the test?" asked Stanley. "You have to find the door by yourself?"

Gertie slipped past her friends and ran her hands against the smooth rock wall. "No," she said. "Finding the door is the easy part. Working it? Now that's going to take some courage."

"Time out," said Stanley. "What's all that about a dead man?"

"I'm almost positive it's an allusion to a dead man's switch," said Gertie, still running her fingers along the wall. "Felix and I installed one in the haunted house we built in my garage last year. Felix, explain it to the man."

Felix looked concerned. "Well, typically levers are called 'dead man's switches' when they take constant pressure to operate. If the operator releases the pressure, for whatever reason, the switch stops working. It's a failsafe mechanism. First came about with electronic streetcars when people were worried that if something happened to the drivers there would be no way to stop the runaway cars."

"Oh," said Charlotte, "like how my riding lawnmower turns off automatically when it senses I'm not in the seat anymore?"

Felix nodded. "But in this case, it means someone has to operate the switch and open the door while the others escape."

"Wait," said Stanley. "One of us has to stay behind?"

Felix didn't respond. And Gertie continued searching the wall.

"This one doesn't have to be yours, Gertie," said Herman. "It could be Stanley's."

"I know it's my test," said Gertie, "Because MacBeth is making each of us face our fears."

"You have fears?" said Herman. "Aren't you the one who loves Halloween, and horror movies, and anything scary?"

"That's different," said Gertie. "All that stuff is— as long as I'm with— look, it's stupid, okay."

"As long as you're what?" said Stanley.

"As long as I'm not alone!" snapped Gertie. "Okay, listen, I can act tough around other people, but when I'm alone...I...I'm afraid. Got it? I'm afraid of being left alone."

"I'm sorry," said Stanley. "I didn't know."

"Nobody knows but Felix," said Gertie. "So maybe now we can just drop it and look for the stupid—wait, I think I found it." Gertie pressed her palm on a large stone that slid back easily into the wall and clicked into place. With a loud crack, a doorway opened in the side of the cave thirty feet to her right, just in front of the other kids. Light poured in, and it took a moment for their eyes to adjust to the green island and the blue water a mere ten yards beyond.

"Go!" said Gertie.

"Wait," said Stanley, "what if one of us held it open for the others, then ran through the doorway before it closes?"

Gertie shook her head. "I don't think you understand. If I just take a little bit of pressure off this stone, watch what happens." Gertie let the stone slide back an inch and the heavy door slammed shut so hard the cave trembled around them.

"Wow," said Herman.

"Yeah," she said. "Not worth the risk of Math Inspectors pancakes. And there's no way to wedge the stone in place, either. Listen, I've got to stay here until you guys send help. Which you will do just as fast as humanly possible. Now go before I lose my nerve."

"No," said Felix.

"No, what?" said Gertie.

"I'm not going to leave you here by yourself. I'll do it for you, or we'll do it together."

Gertie's eyes opened wide. "You'd do that for me?"

Felix smiled. "Are you kidding me, Gertie? You're my best friend. You feed me Snickers when my blood sugar's low. You grab things for me from the bottom shelves of the grocery store. And best of all, you tolerate me even when I'm being an idiot. Which is most of the time."

"Felix Dervish, that is the nicest thing you've ever said to me."

"Don't mention it, Short Stuff. Just come over here, and—"

Gertie cut him off. "But I can't."

"You can't?"

"No. The clue says it'll allow *all but one to go through*. We all have our fears to face. If I don't follow the rules and face mine, MacBeth is going to blow up that roller coaster. As a side note, he probably will anyway, and since this seems like as good a time as any, please let me say that I TOLD YOU SO!"

Felix started to walk towards her.

"Stanley," said Gertie. "Get them out of here. You still have your test to face, and you might need everyone's help to do it. I'll be fine. Now go! I'll give it a ten count and let it go, so nobody is tempted to play the hero."

Gertie pressed the stone in place, and the wall started to slide open like the Flintstones' garage door. Stanley took it all in instantly. He motioned to Charlotte, who pulled herself and Herman into the blinding light. Stanley grabbed Felix, who was still trying to get to Gertie.

"Now," said Gertie. "Get him out of here, Stanley!" She released pressure on the stone and the bright daylight started slipping away, foot by foot. Stanley grabbed Felix by the belt buckle and, with a final effort, pulled them both through the collapsing doorway.

CHAPTER FOURTEEN

CLIMBING THE COASTER

Stanley and Felix landed on the grass just in time to hear the loud noise of the rock wall sealing itself closed.

"What are you doing?" screamed Felix. "Gertie! Gertie! Just hold on. Stanley, why did you do that?"

"Because Gertie asked me to, Felix," said Stanley. "She chose to face her fears, just like the rest of us. It was her choice to make. Besides, so far MacBeth has given us a safe way through. Gertie's got the flashlight and canteens. I'm sure she'll be fine till we get back to Mr. Dahlgren's and send help."

"I'm not leaving this island," said Felix. "You do what you want. But I'm not leaving."

Stanley checked his watch. "Okay, Felix. I get it. You stay and lead the cops to the opening at the top of the hill. I'll tell them to bring a ladder. Charlotte, Herman?"

"You're going to need our help to get back as fast as you can," said Charlotte.

Herman nodded.

"Wait for the cops to go back in, Felix," said Stanley. "Promise me." But Felix didn't seem to notice anything his friends said.

The three friends raced to the boat and cast off. The all took turns rowing as fast as they could, and a quarter of an hour later they were back on the mainland and running for the Dahlgren farm. Before they got there several police officers spotted them. Stanley ran up to the first one he could reach and, though out of breath, explained as best he could about Gertie and Felix.

"I'll get on it right away," said the officer.

Just then a cruiser pulled up and the passenger side window slid down. "Get in," said Officer Evans.

Stanley sat up front. "Officer, I'm really sorry we—"

"Later, Stanley. We've got work to do. Tell me you at least got the key while you ran around disobeying direct orders from me, the chief, and probably your parents."

"I'm really sorry—"

"I said save it. Yes or no, do you have it?"

"We do," said Stanley.

Evans snatched his radio. "Johnson to Central. Calling in a 10-49 on county road DD."

"Johnson?" said Charlotte.

"10-49?" said Herman.

Evans motioned for them to strap in. "Usually a 10-49 is a car with a tail light out. Today, it means something a little different." He turned on his lights and siren and peeled out of Dahlgren's. "Please tell me Gertie and Felix are alright."

"I think so," said Stanley. "I sent an officer after them."

The trees and dirt roads passed by in a blur, and soon they reached pavement and buildings. Cars slowed, stopped, or pulled off the road at strange angles as the cruiser turned north and passed a colorful sign telling them their destination was only two miles away. Hamilton Park was surrounded by acres of woods. Stanley searched the horizon until he finally spotted it sticking out over the tree line— the wooden tracks of the Hamilton Roller Coaster. They followed signs for the park, but drove past the parking lot and up to the main entrance.

"Look at all those people," Herman said, pointing at the crowd gathered in the closest lot.

"Yeah," said Evans. "The whole town's probably here by now."

A police barricade was set up in the passenger drop off zone, so Evans pulled as close as he could and put the cruiser into park.

Stanley stepped out of the car and took in the scene with his friends. He looked again at the crowd of people behind the barricade, then up at a gigantic sign above the ticket kiosks that said: Hamilton Park.

Stanley repeated the often heard line that could normally be heard playing on radio commercials this time of year. "Hamilton Park, where all your dreams come true."

"More like all your nightmares," said Herman.

Charlotte pointed up at the video screen that was visible even at this distance. "Where's our smiling friend?" she asked.

Stanley examined it and saw that half of the screen was a live shot of the roller coaster, and the other half was a countdown clock just turning to 15:15. But no MacBeth.

"The big smiley face disappeared as soon as you kids left the park," said Chief Abrams, walking up to the car. "I'm sending the bomb squad in. Where's the key?"

Stanley shook his head. "Won't work, Chief. We may not see him anymore, but MacBeth is watching us. The moment the police go near the roller coaster, he'll blow it."

"I can't send you kids in there," said Chief Abrams.

"Hear me out," said Stanley. "We've got a little less than 15 minutes. If there is one thing I've learned about MacBeth today, it's that he plays by the rules. If I do too, I can save the roller coaster. It'll take me, what, 3 or 4 minutes to reach it? A couple more to diffuse it?"

The chief looked at Stanley hard. "I don't have the same faith in this guy that you do. He's not going to play by anybody's rules but his own."

"Fine," said Stanley. "Let's say I go and something doesn't go as planned. I still have plenty of time to get clear. If I leave now, that is."

Chief Abrams looked at the big screen. 14:45 and counting. He pointed at Stanley. "You have 7 minutes. Then I'm coming in myself and removing you from the park."

Stanley, Herman, and Charlotte didn't wait for him to change his mind. They ran under the welcome sign and jumped through the turnstiles.

They ran past dozens of empty vendor booths, games, and rides before stopping at the smoldering wreckage of Creepy the Clown.

"I'm still trying to be sad about that," said Herman.

Stanley sighed. "I know. But still, anybody that

would do that to poor Felix has to be stopped. Come on, guys, let's cut through the Spinning Coffee Mugs ride."

"It's so strange being here without people," said Charlotte.

"It's strange being here at all," said Herman. "Hanging out with you guys is never boring. I can tell you that."

"We've got to get you out more often," said Charlotte. "Okay, the entrance to the roller coaster is just around this next—"

"I thought you said there were no people here," said Herman.

Stanley stopped so suddenly that the other two ran into him. There, just five feet away from the ticket booth for the Hamilton Roller Coaster, was Mr. Frank Under. He was standing behind a small booth under a large banner that read *The Under Stand: We Understand Wieners. Frank Under, Proprietor and Hotdog Genius.*

"What are you doing in the park?" gasped Charlotte. "Do the cops know you're here?"

"Like I need their permission," spat Mr. Under.

"Now are you going to buy a hotdog, or what?"

"A—hotdog?" said Stanley. "I don't understand—"

"Of course you don't, you simpleton," barked Mr. Under. "*I* am the Under Stand. Just try to use the name and I'll sue! Now if you're not going to buy a hotdog with a frosty mug of Doggie Dew on this steaming hot day, then step aside. You're holding up the paying customers."

"There's nobody else in the entire park," said Stanley in exasperation. "Mr. Under, you need to leave. Maybe you're the only person in the state that doesn't know this, but there are bombs strapped to that roller coaster right behind you. And the ticking clock on the big screen says they're going to go off in 14 minutes."

Mr. Under scoffed, "It'd take more than that to move me off this spot."

"More than bombs?" said Herman.

Mr. Under wiped his brow with a greasy towel. "I'll have you nitwits know that I have been in this very spot selling Under Doggies every summer since before your parents soiled their first diapers. It's the best spot in the whole place, and it's been mine since—"

"Since he was old enough to cheat," screeched a voice from behind them.

Stanley whirled around to see an old lady about Mr. Under's age leaning on a food cart just across the walkway from the roller coaster. She was parked in the shadows of the Aquatic Bumper Car ride, so nobody noticed her until now.

"You see, youngins," she said with a lisp, "you're standing in the presence of a notorious swindler."

"We really don't have time—" began Stanley.

But the old lady didn't seem to hear him. "Under Hoggy there always hogs the prime spot by the roller coaster. It's a goldmine! And how does he do it, you ask? That's the sneaky part. See, there's only two ways of securing food cart locations in this here park. One is the ancient rule of first-come, first-served. But since Ol' Stinky Underpants always lines up a fortnight earlier than any reasonable person would, and since I travel up from the great state of Texas every year, I can't beat him thatta way. The only other way around it is to outsell every other vendor on the first day of the season, which is today. I do that, and the coveted roller coaster spot is mine for the first time ever. Now why don't you kids come on over here and *Remember the Alamode!* We've got a special going on today: The Davy Crockett Brownie Buster. Served in a coon skin cup."

"Don't listen to her," said Mr. Under. "She's crazy. I should know. That humpbacked troll used to babysit me. Now, I don't normally do this, but I'll throw in a litter of deep fried Poodle Puffs if you buy a K-9 Combo Pack."

"You don't understand," said Stanley. "It's not that I don't want your food, it's that I have to diffuse a bomb. Now I advise you both to—"

"Santa Anna Slurpie then?" said the old lady. "Every combo meal comes with your very own replica Bowie knife, while supplies last."

"I feel like I'm in Wonderland," said Charlotte. "Come on, guys, the countdown's at 13 minutes."

"Right," said Stanley. He ran toward the roller coast.

But just before he got there Mr. Under stepped in his way. "You want to ride the coaster? Then you buy something first."

"You can't do that," said Herman.

"Says who?" growled Mr. Under as he snapped his hot dog tongs.

Charlotte was about to step in front of Stanley when she felt a hand on her shoulder. It was the old lady.

"Says Erma Under, Frankie," the old lady lisped. "We may be old foggies now, but I'm still your big sister, you're still my little brother, and I can still kick your rear up and down this boardwalk. Now let them go. They've got a job to do."

For the first time since Stanley could remember, there was a flicker of fear in Mr. Under's eyes. The hotdog vendor murmured something about Old Yeller Bites, but he moved to the side.

The kids flew past him. After a short consideration, they decided to go to the side of the coaster and climb up to the first drop. Three minutes later, they were out of breath and balancing themselves on scaffolding, examining the three large bombs.

Herman wiped his forehead. "As I've already explained, I'm no Science Club geek. But those things look like they could level the whole park."

"Well," said Charlotte, leaning forward, "there's a keypad here, just like we hoped. So, what, do we just enter the code and the countdown stops?"

"Only one way to know for sure," said Stanley, carefully wrapping one arm around a support beam and stretching his other hand out towards the 1 key.

But before he could touch it, something clicked.

And a digital clock started counting down on the small screen of the keypad.

Stanley looked nervously at Herman and Charlotte. "I hope this works."

Just then a familiar voice boomed all around. "Oh good, the Math Inspectors are here to save the day."

CHAPTER FIFTEEN

CLICK, CLICK, CLICK

MacBeth smiled from the jumbo screen behind them once again. Stanley felt suddenly claustrophobic. Like the yellow smiley face was breathing down his neck.

"Well, Stanley," said MacBeth, "here we are at the end of the game. Did you find the key?"

"We have it," said Stanley, his voice shaking, his throat tight.

"Then where is it?" asked MacBeth.

Stanley wiped his forehead. "The key is a number," he said. "A ratio."

"And with 9:20 to spare," said Charlotte as she looked up at the big yellow smiley face. "It's the Golden Ratio. And that reminds me, have you ever heard of the Golden Rule? It wouldn't hurt you to look it up."

MacBeth laughed. A low, rumbling laugh. "Oh, Charlotte. Maybe I *have* heard of it. And maybe that is why we are here today. And maybe it would be wise for *you kids* to remember the Golden Rule in the future. But just now I am more interested in other things. I am very impressed with you, Math Inspectors. Now all you have to do is diffuse the bomb."

"Let's get this thing over with," said Charlotte. "Stanley, punch in the numbers."

Stanley's finger went to button 1—then he paused and looked at his friends. "I want you two to leave. See if you can get the crazy Under siblings to go with you, and get clear of this place."

"We're in this together," Charlotte said.

"That's right," said Herman. "Together."

"Fine," said Stanley. "Then we end this now. One Golden Ratio, coming up." He hovered his finger over the number 1. But he didn't press it.

"Something on your mind, Stanley?" asked MacBeth.

Stanley looked up at the big screen. "I was just wondering. What do you mean *we* would be wise to remember the Golden Rule in the future? That's a little much coming from a person who picks on a bunch of kids that never did anything to him."

The big yellow smiley face continued to beam down on Stanley, unchanged. "You never did anything to me? Hmm. You may not be as smart as I thought, after all."

From the corner of his eye, Stanley saw the keypad flicker. Instead of a countdown clock, other things flashed across the screen. Numbers. Familiar numbers. One was a fraction: *3/8*. The other was a number followed by a comma and another number: *41.77974, -74.16415.*

They flickered back and forth, one after another. They were familiar alright.

But why were they familiar?

And then, all of the sudden, it hit him, and he swallowed hard. *Oh no!*

"But, it-it can't be," Stanley said. "That means— but you're the one who—"

"Yes," said MacBeth. "Now you understand. Good."

"But we didn't even know—" said Stanley

"You didn't even know," boomed MacBeth. "Do you think that matters in this business, Stanley Robinson Carusoe? Then let me spell it out for you: if you play with the big boys, you have to be ready to play hard. Now punch those golden numbers in before you see what playing hard really looks like."

Stanley looked at the small keypad screen. The countdown had returned, each second clicking by more loudly than the last. His hands shook, but he carefully entered each number, saying them aloud to be sure: one-point-six-one-eight-enter...."

For a second it looked like the clock wasn't going to stop. Then it froze at 8:47. Stanley exhaled in relief.

But just as he turned his back, the loud clicks started again. Stanley looked at the little screen. The countdown was still going.

"Wait, what's going on?" said Charlotte.

Click, click, click went the seconds.

Stanley turned to MacBeth and yelled, "We got the key—you said we did!"

"But not everyone has passed a test yet." MacBeth

said innocently. "And now is the time for Stanley to make his choice."

"What do you mean, make a choice?" said Stanley.

"Think back, Stanley. Everyone else had to take a test today and face their fears. Did you think yours was the math problem at the fountain? Come now, Stanley, math is not what you fear. Math is where you live. Logic is what you love. But what you hate, what you really fear, is having to make decisions where math and logic cannot give you the answer. What you really, really fear is making a choice when the best option is just..."

"A guess," said Stanley as all the air went out of him.

"Precisely," said MacBeth. At that moment, a new image appeared on the big screen.

It was a close up of two wires running from the keypad.

One was red. The other was blue.

"No!" was all Stanley could say.

"Yes," was all MacBeth said in reply.

Stanley dropped his head and examined the

keypad. He could see the two wires connecting it to the bombs.

"To cut the red or to cut the blue...that is the question," said MacBeth.

"Stanley," said Charlotte. "You have to choose."

"I'm sorry," Stanley told his friends. "I've let you down. I have no idea how to solve this riddle."

"Like the man said this morning," said Herman. "Sometimes a riddle is just a riddle. I say we go blue for good luck. It always works for me."

"But if I'm wrong?" said Stanley.

Charlotte put her hand on Stanley's shoulder. "When it counts, you're never wrong."

Stanley swallowed hard, then took Charlotte's pocket knife, reached his trembling hand out towards the two wires...closed his eyes for a moment and said a quick prayer...then opened his eyes, gritted his teeth and said, "But it's not a fair riddle."

Then he snipped the blue wire.

And the timer on the small screen in front of them started to count down in double time.

Click, click, click, click, click, click, click, click...

"But we followed the rules!" Stanley screamed at the big screen. "You can't do this!"

MacBeth chuckled. "So what does Stanley do in impossible situations? How does he choose? What does he do when forced to guess? All very instructive, Stanley. Very instructive. But this is not how it ends, dear boy. Now that you understand why I introduced myself today, you know that this is only the beginning of your choices. Whether we see each other again, well, that is entirely up to you. But consider well what you have learned today: I know you better than you know yourselves; I am smarter than you; and I never, ever play fair. For now I bid you all *adieu*."

The smiley face winked. The big screen went blank.

And Stanley was speechless.

Click, click, click, click...

"Come on," Charlotte said frantically. "At this rate we've got 3 minutes till it blows, maybe less."

"We're not going to make it," said Herman. "Wait, Charlotte, look!"

The clicking was very loud now, and when

Stanley looked down the track he finally understood why. It wasn't just the countdown clock that was clicking. An empty roller coaster was slowly climbing towards them.

"It's our only chance," said Charlotte as she pulled Stanley up onto the narrow wooden shoulder of the track above the first drop. "We've got one shot at this," she said. "Coasters pause just for a second right before the first drop. We'll have to be quick."

For a moment they were on top of the park, and the view made Stanley dizzy. The tiny platform had barely enough room for all three of them, but they weren't on it long before the roller coaster crested.

"Now," said Charlotte.

Stanley felt his friends grab him by the arms, and they jumped into the front car together. Stanley landed in the first seat next to Charlotte, and Herman dove safely into the one behind it.

Charlotte pulled the safety bar down just as they plummeted.

"This ride takes about a minute and a half," Charlotte screamed in Stanley's ear. "That'll be cutting it really close if we want to be clear of the explosion. We'll have to make a run for it as soon as it stops."

Stanley held onto the safety bar for dear life as the Hamilton Roller Coaster made what was probably its very last run.

When the coaster pulled into the station, the kids

yanked their safety bars up and bolted for the exit.

"The water," yelled Herman. And Stanley understood.

Charlotte grabbed Erma, the boys took hold of Mr. Under, and they all went running towards the Aquatic Bumper Cars.

Just as they hit the water, something went boom!

Stanley wasn't sure if being submerged during an explosion was actually helpful, but they didn't seem to have any other choice. And he didn't know how long they should stay underwater either. He looked at the bright colors above the surface and tried to force himself to wait. Before long, though, his lungs felt like they were going to burst, and he swam up.

As soon as his head broke the water, he was showered with the aftermath of the bomb. Stanley turned and saw that he Herman, Charlotte, Mr. Under, and Erma were all covered, too. In bright, beautiful, sparkly confetti.

And the Hamilton Roller Coaster was still there in all its glory. The nation's oldest wooden roller coaster stood like it always had. Practically perfect. Untouched.

Herman coughed. "They weren't real bombs?"

Charlotte wiped confetti out of her eyes. "It was a game. It was all a big stupid game."

Stanley let out a deep breath. "I really, really hate that guy."

Chief Abrams rushed to the side of the pool, and Officer Evans dove in to help the Mr. Under and his sister, Erma.

"Everyone alright?" asked Evans.

Stanley and his friends said they were. So did Erma. Mr. Under just growled "I've got weiners to sell."

"How did you manage to get that roller coaster to us?" Stanley asked Evans.

"It wasn't me," he said. "Better ask your friend here."

"Guilty as charged," said Erma. "It looked like you kids needed my help. So I left my cart just long enough for Blunder Doggie to steal half of my coon skin cups. But it worked."

"You can't prove a thing," said her brother as he spat on his fingers and smoothed out his eyebrows.

The kids were attended to by medical personnel

at the side of the pool. Stanley had a bump on his head from the jump into the roller coaster, and Herman had a scratch on his arm from assisting Mr. Under into the pool.

"Have you heard anything from Gertie and Felix?" asked Charlotte.

"Just got a call from my officers out at the island," said the chief. "Sounds like the moment the confetti bombs went off, Gertie came shooting out of the cave on some sort of a water slide. Actually, I hear she enjoyed it. Seems she and Felix refused to leave until they each got to ride the slide half a dozen times."

"Just watch," said Herman, "Felix will want to turn the place into a water park."

"Right now it's a crime scene," said the chief. "From what we can make out, it sounds like it was a smuggler's cave. Probably a place MacBeth used to store contraband before selling it on the black market. But it's cleared out, so hopefully that means he's pulled out of the area too. You kids shouldn't have to worry about him again."

Stanley looked thoughtful, but he didn't say anything.

Then he said, "Chief, I think you need to pick up Dr. Know-It-All for questioning. I've tried to keep my mind clear all day, but I can't help thinking that he's got to be MacBeth. He took off for lunch mid-morning. He works in riddles that are just completely unfair choices. And then there's the whole colored wire thing—"

"Way ahead of you," said the chief. "We had a hunch about him, too. We went by his place soon after you left the park."

"Let me guess," said Charlotte, "he wasn't there?"

Chief Abrams nodded. "And nobody around here has ever heard of him before, either. Mr. Hamilton's not even sure how he got a spot in the park. There's no record of him anywhere. But that also means we have no lead on where he could be."

"But he's MacBeth, right?" said Herman.

"Maybe," the chief shrugged. "Won't know till we catch up with him. *If* we catch up with him."

"We'd better get ahold of our parents," said Charlotte.

"They're just outside the barrier," said Evans. "But they looked like they were going to break it down when I left them. Is there anything else you need?"

"No," said Stanley. "Oh wait, there is one thing. Tell all the officers before they leave today to buy something from *Remember The Alamode*. We owe Erma big time."

CHAPTER SIXTEEN

THE FINAL CHOICE

Gertie's round face popped through the trap door. "I hate him."

"Hate who?" said Felix.

"MacBeth," said Gertie.

"I know," said Felix. "I just like to hear you say it." He gave her a hand up and they both walked over to the couch where Stanley and Herman were already waiting.

"Any word on your future?" she asked Herman.

He shook his head. "Chief Abrams told me this morning that in light of my help on the MacBeth case, he wouldn't be telling anyone... at least not yet."

"Not yet?" asked Stanley.

Herman nodded gravely. "He said this would be my motivation to make sure those Jekyll crimes never happen again. Which they won't. If my parents find out, I'll be in Military School the next day."

"It wouldn't be the same around here without you always pulling weird things out of your cargo pants," said Felix.

Herman smiled, reached into his pockets, and threw Felix a Jell-O cup.

"Where's Charlotte?" asked Gertie.

"From the sounds of it," said Stanley, pointing with his chin, "right there."

Charlotte's head appeared in the middle of the tree house floor.

"Did you get it?" asked Stanley.

"Not exactly," said Charlotte, pulling herself effortlessly into the tree house. Her face was grave. "Turns out the Hamilton Award went to the English Club."

"What?" said Stanley. "But how could that—"

Charlotte cut Stanley off. "I swung by Mr. Hamilton's office like you asked, Stanley, and he did ask me to send his thanks for all we did yesterday."

The kids all tried to smile.

"Well, at least there's the toy store cash," said Herman.

"Yeah," said Charlotte. "Oh, and he asked me to give you these, too."

She pulled an envelope from her back pocket and tossed it on the couch next to Stanley. He picked it up and five bracelets fell out. He pushed the glasses up the bridge of his nose and examined them more closely. "Are these season passes to Hamilton Park?"

Charlotte shook her head. "Nope. Those are lifetime passes to Hamilton Park!"

Felix screamed.

Charlotte laughed. "Mr. Hamilton was actually *very* thankful for what we did yesterday. These babies are lifetime Line-Cutters, too. No waiting on any ride, ever again. Although, they don't work for food," she said to Felix.

"That's okay," he said as slipped the bracelet on. "There's always funnel-cake-eating contests. Besides, now that Stanley has had his first taste of the roller coaster and we can all go together, even the loss of Creepy will be softened."

"I never asked you about your first ride, Stanley," said Gertie. "Was it everything you'd hoped it would be?"

"To tell you the truth," laughed Stanley, "considering the situation and all, I don't remember a thing about it."

Felix jingled his bracelet. "Then I say we head over there and do it again for the first time."

"Wait," said Gertie. "I get the idea we were called here today for something else. Spill the beans, Stanley. What do you got for us?"

"There *is* something," said Stanley. "It seems we have a choice to make. An important one. Maybe the most important one we've ever made."

The tree house was silent.

Stanley got up and walked to the window. "When we were up there on the roller coaster yesterday, MacBeth showed me something. He showed me numbers."

"Like the countdown numbers?" asked Felix.

Stanley turned and faced his friends. Then he

went to the whiteboard and picked up a marker. "Like these numbers." Stanley wrote *3/8*. Then he wrote *41.77974, -74.16415.*

Gertie jumped up. "Wait a second, I recognize those. They're important numbers from the Claymore Diamond and the Grinch cases. How does MacBeth know that?"

Felix scratched his chin. "What are you saying? Those crimes were related?"

Stanley nodded. "But that's not the worst of it. MacBeth said we should remember the Golden Rule. Guys, I think MacBeth is—"

"You've gotta be kidding me," said Charlotte. "MacBeth was involved in the Claymore Diamond? And he—wait, MacBeth is the Grinch?"

Stanley nodded. "It seems we've been messing up his plans, and he didn't like it. Yesterday was about doing to us what we've been doing to him."

"Do you think we could write Mr. MacGrinch a nice letter explaining that Polly Partridge was really the one who solved those cases?" said Gertie.

"So let me get this straight," said Felix. "MacBeth was going to buy and resell the stolen Claymore

Diamond on the black market. Then he planned to ruin a bunch of kids' Christmases to pull off a big heist. We stop him, and that whole thing yesterday was about revenge? He put us through the torment of our own worst fears for revenge? HE MADE ME TOUCH SQUIRRELS FOR REVENGE?!?!?"

Felix's face was now the same color as his hair. Gertie pulled out a Snickers and stuffed it in his mouth. He fell quietly back to the couch.

"That could have been part of it," said Stanley. "This MacBeth is some kind of a big time crime boss. He had his own island, for goodness sake. But there's no way he did all that just for revenge. First, the tape recorder in the cave said that the morning's riddles were very 'instructive,' and that the tests for each of us would be even more 'instructive.' Then MacBeth said the same thing about watching me squirm when there was no way to stop the bombs. I think it was a practical exercise. He was testing our response. But I bet he was testing the response of the cops, too. Which means he's probably planning something else around here. Maybe something big. But there's another reason, too."

"Why else would he do it?" asked Gertie.

Stanley shrugged. "It's just a hunch, but I think he was trying to give us a way out."

"Meaning what?" said Herman.

"Meaning we've had a good run at being detectives this past year. But now we have a decision to make. It turns out this job is way more dangerous than any of us first expected the day we plugged in the police scanner. We've made enemies. One is a really powerful enemy. I wanted to call you all here today and give you the chance to bow out. There'd be no shame in us quitting now. We'd have the good memories of our 6th grade year. Nobody could take that from us."

"Like I'm going to let a bully like MacBeth tell me what I can do," said Gertie, cracking her knuckles.

Stanley held up his hand. "Wait a minute. This is serious. The last thing MacBeth said was that he's *not going to play fair*. We've been warned, and the next time something like this happens, there won't be confetti involved. Think about what he put us through yesterday."

The tree house went quiet for a long time.

Then Charlotte stood up. "See, and that's where I think he made his big mistake," she said. "There are different ways to look at what MacBeth did yesterday. One way is this—he took a bunch of kids and tormented them with their worst fears. But the other is this—he took a bunch of detectives and made them face their worst fears. He thought he was scaring us off. I'm not so sure he did. I think he showed us just how tough we really are."

"So what do you say?" asked Stanley. "Because if we take on one more case, we help the cops out a single time, we so much as consult on an investigation, maybe just maybe we've made ourselves fair game to whatever MacBeth can throw our way."

Just then a knock came on the trap door. When Felix opened it a mass of curls pushed through the opening in the floor. The tear-stained face that followed belonged to a friend of Stanley's little sister.

"Felicia," said Stanley, "what's wrong?"

"It's Mr. Tippins," said the girl.

"Your rat?" said Stanley.

The girl nodded, then broke into tears. "Blaise said he gave you my letter. Did you read it?"

Stanley looked guilty. "I'm sorry. I put it in my pocket yesterday, and it took a plunge in the Aquatic Bumper Cars. You better just tell us about it."

Felicia dried her eyes. "My mom is convinced Mr. Tippins is breaking out of his cage at night and eating all our crackers in the pantry. I know it isn't him, but she said she's going to give him away. If anybody could prove his innocence it's you, Math Inspectors. My brother told me you were busy and not to bother you, but will you help me?"

Stanley looked at his friends. "Well?"

Charlotte nodded.

Herman gave him a thumbs up.

Felix cupped his hands over his head and waved them.

Gertie put her arm around the little girl. "You've come to the right place, darling. But first let me ask you a question. Do you know where Polly Partridge lives?"

"Sure, just a few houses down from me."

"And do you have any pies in your house?"

"Like coconut cream?"

"Exactly like coconut cream. Listen Felicia, we'll take your case but it's gonna cost you."

"How much?"

Gertie leaned down and whispered into the little girl's ear. Felicia's eyes widened and she broke into a huge smile. Then she held her hand out and Gertie shook it. "You've got yourself a deal."

Felix shouted. "Because we're the MATH INSPECTORS!" He jumped up into the air, tried to do the multiplication symbol, hit the back of the couch, did a summersault, and landed flat on his back.

Gertie patted Felix on the head. "Did you *mall* down, you Big Red Bean Pole?"

Stanley laughed, walked to the trap door, and opened it. "Come on, Math Inspectors. It appears that the game is afoot."

THE END

DO YOU WANT TO LEARN MORE ABOUT THE MATH INSPECTORS?

You can find all books in The Math Inspectors series at Amazon http://www.amazon.com/dp/B00O2AMVW4/

or you can visit our website at www.TheMathInspectors.com.

CAN YOU HELP US SPREAD THE WORD ABOUT THE MATH INSPECTORS?

If you enjoyed reading about Stanley, Charlotte, Gertie, Felix, and Herman, we would be honored if you asked a parent to help you write a short review about our book on Amazon. Those honest reviews really help readers find our books, and we want to introduce The Math Inspectors to as many readers as possible. Thank you so much!

Daniel Kenney & Emily Boever

DO YOU HAVE WHAT IT TAKES TO BE A MATH INSPECTOR?

Hey guys! If this isn't your first Math Inspectors mystery, then you know who this is. Yep, it's your favorite Math Inspector Gertie!

Stanley asked Felix and me a long time ago if we would "help" him come up with word problems, so kids everywhere could sharpen their own detective skills. Luckily for Stanley, I'm really good at these things, so I don't mind the fact that he hasn't lifted a single math finger to help us. Not once. Not ever.

And luckily for me, word problems are easy to come up with. I mean, they're all around us. Most of us solve them all the time and don't even realize it. Take Felix and me for example. We're here at the tree house today discussing something important that only math can help us decide. We've both agreed to come up with a proposal for a summer business we can run together. We'll split the initial startup costs, so the big question is this: *Which business will bring in more money?* Take a look at the math below, and help Felix and me decide which business to open.

Please note: all taxes are included in the prices below.

Word Problem 1—Felix's Business Proposal: *Fertie's Cat Wash Co.*

Math problem: If Fertie's Cat Wash Co. charges $5.00 per wash, how much money will we make per cat wash after paying for our business costs? Round up to the nearest cent when necessary.

<u>Business Costs</u>
Plastic tub: Free, if Buckets doesn't mind sharing his.
Cat shampoo: $3.25 per bottle. Each bottle contains enough for 10 washes.
Drying towel: Free from Felix's closet. Each towel

will cost 25 cents to clean. Each cat will use 1 towel. Ribbons: $2.50 per bag. Each bag contains 25 ribbons. Each cat gets 1 ribbon. Kitty Treats: $5.20 per box. Each box contains 39 organic kitty treats. Each cat gets 1 treat. Cuddles: Free, if Buckets doesn't mind sharing his.

Hi guys, it's Felix here. Gertie says cats don't like water. This is the first I've heard of it, since my own adorable ball of fur, Buckets, absolutely loves water. We go swimming in Lake Ravensburg all the time. All I have to do is put birthday cake on a raft, and Buckets will swim miles to get it. So I think the cat wash idea is a Cash Cow, and hopefully you'll agree once you've done the math.

Because I'm so certain of it, here's a follow up question. Maybe we'll just stroll over to another part of the tree house so I can give it to you in secret.

Word Problem 2—Felix's Follow Up

Mr. Hamilton is raising money to replace Creepy the Clown (I know, yippee!). Gertie never loved

Creepy, so I don't want to say anything in front of her, but anybody who donates $1000 gets their name engraved on the side of one of the coaster cars (I know, double yippee!).

Help me figure out the math on this.

Hint: Gertie is not participating in my Creepy dream, so just use my earnings to do your calculations.

Math Problem: Using your answer from world problem 1, how many cats would I need to bathe before I earn $1000? BONUS QUESTION: If I could actually find Cows made of Cash, that would be a lot easier than having to run a business. How valuable are these mythical creatures, and how many Cash Cows would I need to find to reach my goal of $1000?

It's Gertie again. Why do I even humor Felix and his crazy ideas? A cat wash? And who would do business with a place called Fertie's?

It's time to get serious and talk about why we've

really gathered in the tree house today. Here's my proposal to cool the people of Ravensburg down during the hot days of summer. I've gone ahead and calculated the cost of each ingredient for a single serving. That should make your job a lot easier.

Please Note: all taxes are included in prices below.

Word Problem 3—Gertie's Business Proposal: *Gerlix's Smoothie Stand*

Math Problem: If Gerlix's Smoothie Stand charges $2.00 per serving, how much profit will we make on each flavor of smoothie? Round up to the nearest cent if necessary.

Smoothie 1: Orange You Glad It's Summer?
Orange sherbet: $.75
Limeade: $.30
Crushed ice: $.05
Cup: $.06

Smoothie 2: Santa's On Vacation

Vanilla ice cream: $.80

Peppermint candy: $.10

Almond milk: $.35

Cup: $.06

Smoothie 3: How Felix Gets His Veggies

Oreos: $.20

Chocolate Ice Cream: $.90

Coconut Milk: $.35

Kale: $.05

Spinach: $.05

Cup: $.06

Still Gertie talking. Pretty good idea, huh? I'll wait for your mind to stop reeling from the feeling of amazement at my entrepreneurial skills.

Now on to a little follow up question. I sent Felix for a blender and some smoothie ingredients so we could test the products before making our final choice. While he's gone, I'll ask you a problem that it's better he doesn't hear. For his own good, you understand.

Word Problem 4—Gertie's Follow Up

Rumor has it that Mr. Hamilton is considering ditching his plans to rebuild Creepy the Clown and replacing it with a petting zoo (I know, yippee!). True, Felix loved that old clown ride. But let's face it...it *was* creepy. For Felix's own good, I'm planning on donating money for the petting zoo. Anyone who donates $100 gets to have their name engraved on a brick that lines the new pig pen. I'll even have Mr. Hamilton put Felix's name on the brick (instead of mine, because I'm nice like that). So here comes the math.

Please Note: as tempting as it would be to use Felix's money for this project, I won't. He probably has something he's saving up for, too.

Math Problem: If I donate all of my profits from every How Felix Gets His Veggies smoothie we sell, how many Veggie smoothies do I need to sell before I earn $100?

Hi guys. It's your old pal Felix. I've got the tree house to myself for the moment. Here's a free tip:

don't operate your mom's blender without its top on tight. It was horrible. There was kale everywhere. Gertie went home to clean it out of her ears, and I'm going to be here a while scrubbing the tree house. We've decided that maybe we need to rethink our summer business plans. Maybe you can help us. If you find any Cash Cows, please mail directly to:

Felix Dervish

Awesome Tree House

Ravensburg, New York

Oh, and I've got an idea for one last word problem.

Word Problem 5

Math Challenge: Use your Math Inspector's skills to come up with a business proposal yourself.

It could be one that you think we should do. But it could also be one that would be fun for you to do. Whatever it is, share it with your parents, and see what they think about it. If you get your parents' permission, go to our website TheMathInspectors.com and share your plan with other Math fans, too.

While you're thinking, I'll be here scrubbing. But first, let me fix myself another smoothie... Felix out!

ABOUT THE AUTHORS

DANIEL KENNEY

Daniel Kenney is the co-author of the wildly successful Math Inspectors series and the author/illustrator behind the hit series, The Big Life of Remi Muldoon. He has also written such popular books as Pirate Ninja, The Beef Jerky Gang, and Katie Plumb & The Pendleton Gang. Daniel and his wife live in Omaha, Nebraska with zero cats, zero dogs, one gecko, two very lost toads, and a whole flock of kids. When he's not writing or parenting, Daniel pursues his other passion, jet packing around the world. Find more information at www.DanielKenney.com.

EMILY BOEVER

Emily Boever has lived in wondrous places like Germany and Austria, and beautiful places like Naples, Florida. She has taught scholars from Kindergarten through college, coached high school softball, and traveled the U.S. and Europe extensively. But by far, her greatest adventure has been living with her husband, Matt, their gaggle of children, and the world's dumbest-yet-most-lovable dog, Gus, in Nebraska. Emily teaches the kids, works as a part-time professor and tutor, and does most of her traveling these days through books.

CPSIA information can be obtained
at www.ICGtesting.com
Printed in the USA
LVHW04s1618200418
574264LV00002B/419/P